SIX SHOOTER

STANLEY

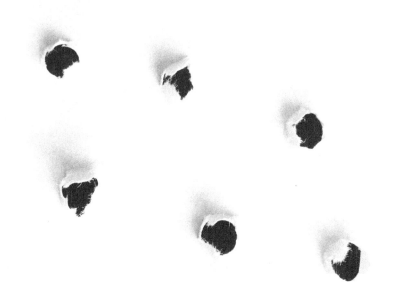

SHORT CRIME STORIES

Martin Stanley was born in Teesside in 1972. He is the author of eleven books (including the one you are holding). His works include *The Gamblers*, a noir thriller set in Bristol, and *The Glasgow Grin*, part of his Stanton brothers' series of crime thrillers. He lives and works in London.

Books by Martin Stanley:

Bad Luck and Trouble
Best Laid Plans
The Green-eyed Monster
Bone Breakers
Noughts and Double Crosses
The Hunters
The Glasgow Grin
Fighting Talk
Dirty Snow (and other stories)
The Gamblers
Six Shooter (short crime stories)

SIX SHOOTER

You Fucking Diamond 5
To The Grave 43
The Accident 51
You're Worth More Than You Think 57
The Carpenter's Arms 71
A Man Called Mary 93

SIX SHOOTER

Martin Stanley

© 2024 Martin Stanley

The right of Martin Stanley to be identified as the author of this work has been asserted by him in accordance with the Copyright, Designs and Patents Act 1988.

This is a work of fiction. All characters and events in this publication are fictitious, and any resemblance to real persons, living or dead, is purely coincidental.

All rights reserved. No part of this book may be reproduced, stored in a retrieval system, or transmitted in any form or by any means electronic or mechanical photocopying, recording or otherwise, without prior permission of the copyright owner.

For Julia and the baby.
You both make me want to be a better person.

For Olive (2015-2024).
The best dog anybody could ever want.
You will never know how much we miss you.

The author would like to thank Keith Nixon for his help with the manuscript.
It's a tighter beast because of your input, mate.

YOU FUCKING DIAMOND

You Fucking Diamond was first published as part of Ryan Bracha's novel of stories *The Thirteen Lives of Frank Peppercorn* in 2017. It was one of the fastest pieces I ever wrote. Ryan needed something in a hurry, which was a problem for me because I rarely write anything quickly. But I did have a Stanton brothers piece called *High Conflict* about them coming to their sister's aid. It was pretty easy to switch out Eric Stanton for Frank and I found it just as simple to drop Derek from the narrative completely.

I did the first draft and the rewrite in a fortnight. I doubt I'll ever finish anything that fast again. But those two weeks were a wild ride of bugger all sleep and a lot of grafting to come up with what you're about to read.

Sadly it was last project Ryan published as a writer, which is a real loss because he possessed an imagination that made him stand out from the crowd. A lot of the indie writers I consider my peers and betters seem to have packed it in over the last few years. The indie scene feels a lot duller these days.

Happily, Ryan has since moved into music, where he seems to be doing well as part of the outfit Misery Prize. I'm not sure if he misses the wild west days when Amazon's Kindle store had rough looking covers and a surfeit of crazy ideas from a bunch of writers who didn't seem to give a fuck.

1.

THE EVENING began in its usual fashion. My husband gave me a backhander across the mouth and followed it up with a blow to the gut for whimpering.

Usually, the reason was a mystery. Maybe Joe's evening cuppa wasn't dark enough? Or maybe I was making too much noise as I tidied his mess? There was always the remote possibility that I hadn't cleaned to his exacting and arcane standards? But sometimes he didn't need an excuse; I was simply in the wrong place at the wrong time.

However, tonight was different. Joe had pulled up in the car park near my office, on his way home from work, and pressed the horn repeatedly until my line manager, Susan, looked up from her screen and turned in my direction. Staring at my old bruises, poorly hidden beneath a thick layer of foundation, she jerked her head towards the exit.

"You'd better go, Mel."

Guilt brought a hot flush to my cheeks. "The Anderson job needs to go tonight."

Susan fixed me with her cold blue gaze and disguised her anger with a fake grin. It was hard to tell if she was angry with my husband or me. She pushed her mouse across the desk with aggressive jerks of her arm and stabbed the button forcefully. The mouse pointer lurched around a double-page spread before finally finding its way to a large column of text.

"It *will* go tonight," Susan said through gritted teeth. "One way or another, but you should go."

She turned back to the screen with a flick of long red hair.

As I made my way to the exit, past several co-workers who avoided my gaze, I peered over my shoulder. I wanted her to know that this wasn't my fault. I wanted her to sense my desperation. I hoped she'd turn, see the fear in my eyes, or my trudging gait, and beg me to stay.

But it wasn't to be. Susan remained hunched towards the screen, smashing at the keyboard with her fingers.

I left the office and exited the building. The evening was warm and clammy, but the sweat running down my back was from fear rather than the humidity. I dabbed my forehead with the back of a hand and walked towards a dented Ford Focus that revved impatiently in the parking area.

A man shouted my name, which made me turn my head.

Harry from accounts approached with my door keys in his hand. He smiled and shook them. "You forgot these."

I returned the smile, even though it was difficult to hold in place. My heart beat rapidly. Another trickle of sweat ran down the gully of my neck.

Joe didn't like it when I talked to other men, particularly ones as handsome, confident, and well dressed as Harry.

This meant trouble.

I thought about looking over my shoulder at Joe. I needed to know how much of a problem this was. But I also knew that this would make me seem even more guilty. Instead, I moved back to the doorway and plucked the keys from Harry's grasp. As I began to make a quick getaway, Harry put his right hand on my shoulder.

"There's a few people from the office going for drinks tomorrow, if you fancy it?"

Talking with another man was bad enough, but any physical contact made Joe furious, no matter how innocent it was. Panic set in. I began crafting best- and worst-case scenarios in my head. If I was lucky, he wouldn't bruise me too badly.

I shook off Harry's hand, saying: "Got stuff to do, sorry."

He shrugged his powerful shoulders and adjusted his tie. "Well, at least have a think about it."

"I've gotta go," I replied, hitching a thumb in the direction of the car. "Thanks for the keys."

I kept the happy expression on my face and hoped it appeared genuine enough to fool my husband. The car's engine increased in volume as I approached. Smoke poured from the exhaust and formed dark clouds.

I opened the door and climbed into the front passenger seat. The interior reeked of the bitter engine oil that wafted off Joe's grey overalls. I tried not to cough.

I directed a smile at Joe, but it wasn't returned. His small blue eyes burned with loathing. His oil-stained hands had a white-knuckled grip on the steering wheel. His teeth ground together with an unpleasant rasp. The sound seemed to fill the car. He waited a long time before speaking:

"Who the fuck was that?"

"That's just Harry," I replied with a shrug. "I forgot my keys."

I jangled them for emphasis.

Joe's eyes narrowed. "And what's *Harry* doing with your keys?"

"I left them on my desk," I said, "in my rush to leave the office."

Joe sneered. "Rush? I don't seem to recall any rush; considering you've made me wait here, like a cunt, for the last ten minutes."

I let my hands drop on my lap. I wrapped my fingers around the keys and clutched them until the hard edges cut into my flesh. Looking down, I feigned humility the way my husband liked and murmured sorry into my chest. Doing it made me feel dirty, but it was necessary. It might save me from a more brutal beating when we arrived home.

"Sorry. I – I genuinely thought I was rushing."

The engine revved.

"Maybe next time you should actually rush instead of just talking about it."

"You're right. It won't happen again."

Joe gave me a smug grin. "It better not."

We drove home in silence. Occasionally we craned our heads to stare at refurbished Victorian terraces with fancy sash windows and expensively cleaned brickwork and dreamed of better lives. Joe couldn't help but stare enviously at the expensive cars that sat outside their front doors. Driving down Highgate's narrow high street, we cast admiring glances at its clean, village-style shop fronts.

Then we moved past the hospital, and Archway station, and accelerated down Holloway Road. The shop fronts were dirtier and less well-tended. Kebab joints and dirty chicken outlets mingled with betting shops and charity stores. Joe looked at the buildings with a glum expression.

Halfway down the road, we turned left and made our way down a street of beautiful brownstone terraces and attractive redbricks. Then we turned left again and picked up speed until we drove into an unappealing estate of low-rise flat blocks. Joe pulled into an unused parking space and turned off the engine.

Fearing a quick backhander, I drew back instinctively.

Joe smirked. "If I was gonna smack you one, I'd've already done it."

We got out of the car and walked across a patch of grass to our block. Then we went inside and took the elevator to the third floor. Neither of us said anything in the lift. I kept my gaze on the floor, but I didn't need eyes to feel Joe watching me. Goosebumps dotted my bare forearms. I suppressed the urge to shiver.

The lift pinged open, and we marched down the corridor, with Joe leading the way. I remained two steps behind — he didn't like me taking the lead in anything. Joe unlocked the door of our flat and went inside. I followed him into the living room.

That's when he caught me with the backhander.

His knuckles mashed my lips against my teeth. It was the shock more than the pain that made me whimper. But Joe didn't like whimpering. He shuffled forward and slammed a low right into my gut that folded me forward. The pain left me coughing for breath; the shock made me lose control of my bladder. I dropped on my knees in a puddle of piss that was rapidly cooling on the hardwood floor and looked up at my husband.

Joe's face was red with anger, and maybe a little excitement, too. He bounced on his toes, his fists tight like he was fighting in the ring.

"D'you fuck him?" he hissed.

I drew in a deep breath and managed to gasp: "What?"

"You heard me, bitch."

He came in close and I instinctively drew away. My pain began to fade, and was quickly replaced with humiliation. Tears spilled down my cheeks as I scrambled to make the situation better.

"Harry's gay," I said, avoiding Joe's gaze.

Harry wasn't gay, but for the sake of this conversation he had to be — if only to save me from a worse beating. Evening light from the window glistened on the piss puddle. Then my husband's shadow blocked everything out, and I looked up.

Joe gave me a grin full of small teeth, worn down by constant grinding. "Gay, straight — it all means the same thing to a slut like you. Bet his cock feels just fine when it's inside you."

Joe crouched and scrutinised me for the slightest blush, the merest flicker of guilt, or anything else he needed to justify hitting me again.

I wiped away tears with my forearm and sniffled. "I never touched him. I promise."

"Promise? You haven't got the slightest fucking clue what a promise means. Fucking wedding vows mean nothing, do they?"

I let out a wail of frustration. "I never cheated on you. Not with him, not with anyone."

Joe's face twitched momentarily. The cogs in his head seemed to whir into life. His eyes widened as if he'd discovered some shocking secret. "You said 'with anyone'."

"I don't understand."

He leant down until his face was just a few inches away. I resisted the temptation to draw back, which would only compound my guilt, at least in his eyes.

"Why'd you specifically use the term with anyone?"

"I… I…"

"I don't remember asking if you'd fucked anyone else," he whispered.

"What are you saying?"

"No," he said with a shake of the head. "What are you saying? I only asked if you fucked Harry. But when you denied it, you brought a whole bunch of other people into it. Fucking anyone."

The hairs on the back of my neck stood upright and I let out a small sob of fear. I was going to die tonight. It was in Joe's eyes, the continuous left-right movement of his jaw, the scrape of his grinding teeth, and the hunched tension in his shoulders. Nothing I could say would change the outcome because words were useless now. Joe's brain had transformed my denial of infidelity into an acknowledgement of multiple affairs. There was only one thing that mattered to him, and this was that he'd married a cheat. It didn't matter that he was the only one who had broken our wedding vows on numerous occasions. All that counted were my many imagined infidelities.

Five years of marriage went through my head in seconds. Soft slaps to the face on our honeymoon for looking where I shouldn't, followed by whispered apologies that always ended with the explanation that it was my fault. Pulled punches to the gut for daring to express an opinion. Blows that got harder as time passed, for reasons that became ever less apparent, followed by rough 'make-up' sex that happened whether I wanted it or not. All of it leading inevitably to this point — the night of my murder.

Unless I took a stand and fought back.

A quick right flashed through the air. The impact snapped my head back. My left cheek burned and throbbed. Vast constellations of stars appeared and died before my eyes. I felt his left hand on my throat, then his right, the fingers tightening, pressing down, cutting off my air supply.

Fear prevented me from reacting. The irrational part of my brain denied what was happening. A voice in my head told me that this wasn't murder; it was all a misunderstanding. Maybe the best thing to do was to surrender and go with it. Relax and let things happen.

Then my adrenaline levels spiked.

Panic and self-preservation kicked in.

Bucking and writhing and twisting my body, I attempted to get free of Joe's grasp. I slapped him and raked my nails down his face. The harder I fought, the tighter he gripped my neck. There was darkness at the edge of my vision that spread ominously towards the centre. Sounds became dull and faint and only my husband's voice carried any weight. I figured I had a few seconds of fight left.

With all my strength, I kicked out and smashed my stiletto heel into Joe's kneecap and ground it in deep. A piercing scream filled my ears. His grip loosened, and I kicked out again, this time driving my heel deep into his thigh muscle. There was another shriek and Joe fell backwards.

I scrambled away on my hands and knees. Joe tried to follow, but slipped in the piss and slammed face first against the floor. He lay there for a few seconds, groaning, as I struggled to my feet. Dizziness scrambled my vision momentarily but, fuelled by adrenaline and anger, I slapped my face until the pain brought me back around. I was still on the verge of collapse but, damn it, I wasn't going down again without a fight.

Joe used the kitchen worktop to help him to his feet. He seemed unsteady.

I removed my stilettos and held them like weapons.

"I'm leaving," I said.

"The fuck you are."

I lurched forward a couple of steps, expecting Joe to rush at me, but something surprising happened. He shuffled back a few inches. It wasn't the distance that amazed me but the look in his eyes. For the first time in our relationship, I noticed fear and doubt. He stepped forward again and winced as he brought his right leg down.

My gaze went to the kitchen. That was my escape route. I locked eyes with Joe again, letting him think I was going to run right through him. If I was lucky, I might be able to wrong-foot him.

"I'm leaving," I repeated. "You can either get outta my way, or I'm gonna put you down." I swiped the air with my shoe to show that I wasn't bluffing.

Joe grinned. "Then I guess you're gonna have to put me down."

I ran at him with a high scream, holding my right shoe high.

Joe's eyes widened. He hesitated a moment. Then he sprung forward and caught me as I swerved right towards the kitchen. Our bodies slammed against the tall fridge-freezer. Something walloped my solar plexus, but I ignored the pain and swung my right arm. The heel smashed into Joe's left eyebrow and tore off a flap.

Panicking, he stumbled back as blood streamed into his eye. He tried to wipe it away. Then, realising how futile this was, he wiped at the sweat that was blinding his other eye.

He couldn't see.

Now was my chance.

I swung again with everything I had.

This time the stiletto crunched against his windpipe.

Eyes bulging, Joe gurgled and clawed at his throat with both hands. He staggered back towards the sink and flapped his mouth uselessly. There was panic on his face. He was trying to take in air, but nothing was getting past the dent where his Adam's Apple used to be. He tried crying for help, but that just made things worse. His face went from red to purple, and his hands flailed around like he was trying to pull oxygen into his body. Gradually, his movements slowed and he fell on the floor. But Joe kept fighting the inevitable, leaving me to wonder if he might heal himself through willpower alone.

But there was no coming back from this.

Face now the colour of a bruise, mouth opening and closing like a fish out of water, Joe lay on his back and stared at the ceiling. Fresh tears soaked the hair near his temples. Piss darkened the crotch of his jeans. Then he stopped moving and his body loosened. The stench of shit hit my nose.

Afraid of getting too close, I craned forward for a better look.

Joe gazed blindly at a point far beyond the ceiling. The irrational thought that he was just playing dead made me skitter back in alarm.

But he wasn't playing, he was just dead.

I dropped the stiletto and began panicking.

I'd killed my husband.

I squatted on my haunches and took deep breaths. How was I going to get out of this? Muttering Oh God like a mantra, I buried my face in my folded arms and thought about the future. I was just about composed enough to know that it wasn't murder. But a voice in my head that sounded like Joe said: *Maybe you can convince them it's self-defence; otherwise it's manslaughter. You're going to prison, you idiot.*

Loud knocking jarred me out of my trance.

A heavy fist shook the door.

"You two better open this door now, or I'll kick a hole in it," said a rough voice. It was our next-door neighbour, Frank. He'd complained about us several times in the past.

One day, after Frank's last complaint went nowhere, my husband went next-door to teach him a lesson. He came back fifteen minutes later covered in blood and bruises, shaking with fear and shock. He didn't hit me for several months afterwards and never spoke about what happened.

Heart thumping, I took slow steps towards the door. I slid the security chain into place and tried to think of a plan. The only thing I came up with was to convince Frank that everything was fine and then decide what to do about my husband's corpse. The ridiculousness of that thought made me giggle for a moment. Then, without warning, my emotional pendulum swung the other way and tears warmed my cheeks. I tried composing myself.

My hand trembled as I opened the door.

"Hello?"

"Don't gimme the hello treatment, miss," he said. "Do you know how much noise you were making?"

Frank came close to the gap. For the first time, I noticed the grey in his hair and the web of lines around his eyes. I'd always imagined him to be in his late thirties, but at this distance I knew he was at least a decade older than that. His eyes studied my face. He gritted his teeth.

"What has that bastard done to you?"

"It's okay," I insisted.

Frank shook his head. "The hell it is. Have you seen your face?"

"No."

"Well, I have," he said. "And it looks a mess."

"They're just tear tracks."

There was a wry smile at the corner of his mouth. "Is that a medical condition?"

"Is what a medical condition?"

"Having such strong tears that they leave bruises behind."

"It's mostly mascara."

"Hmm, bruise coloured mascara. That's a first. Next you'll be telling me that all that blood around your mouth is some lipstick called Scarlet Dream."

"Look, please…"

"Don't please me, just let me in."

I had difficulty swallowing. "Why?"

"Because I wanna have words with Joe."

My eyes turned to the kitchen, then back to Frank.

"He went out."

"No, he didn't."

"But…"

"I've been watching your door for the last five minutes," he said. "And believe me, I'd like to think I'd notice a little detail like that piece of shit skulking off to the pub."

"He's calmed down now."

In fact, he was very calm, almost too calm. I stifled another giggle with the palm of my hand. Frank noticed and squinted his eyes.

"That's nice for him. And what makes you think I've calmed down?"

"Look, Mr…"

"Peppercorn."

"I'll talk to him."

"Of course you will," he said, "but not until I've spoken to him."

"Please go away."

"Why?"

"Because I'm asking nicely."

Frank nodded. "I remember asking you nicely on several occasions to stop making so much noise."

"And I'm sorry about that."

"The time for sorry has long gone," he said, coming even closer. "Now you either open this door, or I'll kick it off its hinges."

Nothing I said or did was having an effect. Frank wasn't going away anytime soon. The longer we had this conversation, the more likely it was that other neighbours might decide to get involved. I wondered if Frank's reluctance to leave had anything to do with their last scuffle.

"Why?"

"Joe knows why."

As I thought about what to say next, Frank charged and slammed the door with his shoulder. The impact tore the strike plate off the doorframe, pushed the door into my face, and sent me sprawling. Frank hurtled into the room, slipped on the wet floorboards, and landed on his stomach with a thump.

Rubbing my sore cheekbone, I thought about running through the open door and leaving Frank with my husband's body. Instead, I slammed the door shut and turned towards the intruder, who was now on his feet and sniffing his fingers.

"Is this piss?" he asked.

I nodded.

Frank held his hands in the air like a surgeon waiting for sterilised gloves. He directed his attention towards the sink. Then his gaze went down towards the kitchen tiles. It was obvious what he saw: the discarded stiletto shoe and my husband's feet. He looked at me with unblinking eyes, then returned his focus to the ground.

Relief washed over me. I no longer felt afraid. The truth was out there, and there was nothing I could do about it. Once Frank regained his composure, the police would be called, statements would be taken, and my new life would begin. I was ready.

A couple of long strides took Frank into the kitchen area. Eyes firmly fixed on the corpse, he turned on the tap and washed his hands. For a man who'd just discovered a body, his demeanour was remarkably cool

"Was it intentional?" Frank said, his tone unruffled.

"What?"

He turned in my direction. "Your husband. Did you mean to kill him?"

Tears flowed again, I rubbed them away with a forearm. "I just wanted to leave. I just wanted a new life."

Frank turned off the tap. "He wouldn't let you?"

"I think he'd finally decided it was time to get rid of me."

Frank pulled a couple of sheets of kitchen roll from a dispenser hanging near the sink and wiped his hands. He dropped the used tissue in his pocket and pointed at me. "Judging by those marks on your neck, I'd say he nearly succeeded."

I couldn't stop shivering and my teeth chattered continuously. Frank left the kitchen, walked through the living room, and into the bedroom. Moments later he emerged with a thick cardigan that he wrapped around my shoulders. "You're in shock," he said. "It's better to keep warm."

"Are you gonna phone the police?"

Frank eyed me with surprise. "Do you want me to?"

"I killed a man."

He shrugged. "In self-defence."

"He's still dead."

"True, but he was a scumbag."

I allowed myself to smile. "I'm not sure how much that matters in a court of law. Every time he hit me, I defended him or refused to talk to the police. I don't even think he's got a criminal record."

"Then it wouldn't be wise to phone the police, would it?"

"What are you saying?"

Frank smiled. "You seem smart. Figure it out."

Was he suggesting that we bypass the authorities and dispose of the body? A brief flicker of hope allowed me to consider a future again; one where I could have a career and children. Was Frank offering that?

"Let's assume I'm not thinking clearly for a moment."

Frank nodded and strode around the living room. I was surprised at how tall he was. There were times when he'd passed me in the hallway that he seemed barely more than the five-six I came to in high heels. His demeanour was different, more self-assured than the hunched figure I occasionally saw shuffling down the corridor with the bin bags.

"I know people who can dispose of your problem."

"Like who?"

Frank stopped moving briefly, his expression one of almost fatherly concern like he was dealing with a slow-minded child. "Are you really going to ask me that?"

I answered with a silent shrug of the shoulders.

"Let's just say they're the kind of people you don't want to ask questions about."

"Okay, then why're you helping me?"

"I told Joe that if our paths crossed again, I was going to beat him to death. You saved me the trouble."

"Kind of hard not to cross paths," I said, "seeing as we're neighbours."

"Joe knew what I meant."

"Which…"

"Look, stop wasting time," he snapped, holding a mobile phone in the air. "It's time to make the decision."

2.

I GRABBED the handle of the largest suitcase we owned and pulled it down off the top shelf of the wardrobe. I unzipped the case and scattered the contents carelessly around the bedroom. Then I hefted the case into the living room, where Frank was still on the phone, striding back and forth from the sofa to the television.

"It needs to be now, Tone," he said, his voice dropping to a hiss. "Remember something, friend. You owe me. D'you really think you'd be walking the streets today if it wasn't for my intervention? Cal had every intention of putting you in the ground. After everything I've done for you, you're fucking me over... Oh, don't give me that, you are fucking me over. And, you know what? I think I'm gonna tell Cal he can have his way with you... Goodbye, Anthony, I hope he really hurts you."

I walked into the kitchen and placed the case beside my husband. It looked big in the wardrobe and felt even larger in my hand, but beside the corpse, it looked tiny.

Frank chuckled. "Oh, then you can do me that favour, after all? Funny that. You better go open, now, coz if I have to wait, it'll be *you* going into the fucking furnace."

He hung up and looked at me. "Why the long face?"

"See for yourself."

Frank came around the counter and stared at the problem. There was little emotion on his face. "I'm figuring Joe has a toolkit, him being a mechanic and all?"

I nodded.

"Get me the biggest hammer you can find and as many towels as you can spare."

I went to the cupboard by the door and found my husband's tool box. Inside was a large ball-peen hammer that I handed to Frank.

He gazed at it for a moment with what appeared to be admiration. "Towels," was all he said.

A quick recce of the bedroom resulted in me handing Frank five small towels and three large ones. He lined the inside of the case with one of the big towels and placed the other two beneath Joe's right leg. Without looking up, Frank said: "Now turn on some music. Make sure it's loud. But if I hear the Spice Girls or Take That or some other shit, I'm going to go home and leave you to it. Are we clear?"

"Crystal. How does the Stones sound?"

"It depends. Are we talking post-*Exile* or Pre?"

"I can make it *Exile* if you'd like, and work back from there?"

"I'd like that a lot."

Exile on Main Street went into the CD unit, and I turned up the sound. Even so, the volume was still low enough to prevent the upstairs and downstairs neighbours from getting annoyed. The opening guitar riff of *Rocks Off* kicked in. Frank gave me the thumbs up. Then he disappeared behind the unit and raised the hammer high.

As soon as it came down, I turned my back and stared at the CD player. The impact wasn't something I heard so much as sensed in my bones. I fought the urge to vomit, but every hammer blow made that fight a little harder. Sooner or later I was going to lose my composure, and my dinner, so I went into the bedroom and got on the bed. I took off my wet dress, curled into a ball, and wrapped a thick duvet around me. I tried rationalising the events of the evening, that what happened was self-defence, that Joe was a wife-beating adulterer and alcoholic, but I couldn't get past the reality that I'd taken a life. In spite of everything else, Joe was still a human being and there had once been love in our relationship, no matter how twisted it might have been. He might have been a terrible person, but Joe deserved better than to be folded into a suitcase.

I sobbed into the bedding until it was damp, then I fell asleep.

Frank woke me with a gentle prod. Something about my expression must have carried a hint of a scream because he placed his big hand over my mouth and shook his head.

"Take a deep breath. You're fine."

His palm smelled of handle rubber, metal and bleach, but beneath them was the coppery under-scent of blood. I didn't want to breathe in those odours and have them become my abiding memory of Joe. Even now, after all the beatings and the abuse, I found excuses for his behaviour. Deep down I still blamed myself. Joe's words still carried weight: *If you'd kept your gaze to yourself, this wouldn't have happened. If you'd just done what I told you, I wouldn't have smacked you one, would I? If you watch your tone in future, then maybe I'll watch my fucking hands.*

I refused to breathe, and my face turned red. I struggled and tried to pull the hand away, but Frank increased the pressure on my face. "I'm not letting go until you give me the sign. Now breathe."

Finally, I accepted that this night was going to be my abiding memory of Joe and took a deep breath through my nose. Frank removed the hand and stepped back.

"Are you calm?"

I nodded. "How long was I asleep?"

"Long enough for me to finish the job and clean up. But now it's time for you to clean up," he said, hitching a thumb over the shoulder, in the direction of the bathroom. "We have to make this look right."

I began stripping off my underwear shyly. I figured this was the way that Frank wanted me to repay him.

His alarmed expression told me otherwise. He waved his hands frantically. "I didn't mean you should get naked in front of me. I'm not like your fucking husband. Go get changed in the bathroom. You can give me your undies when you're finished."

I removed my bra and knickers in the bathroom and studied my reflection in the mirror. My lips and left cheek were swollen. Finger marks covered my neck. They were already beginning to bruise. No amount of make-up was going to disguise Joe's final handiwork. Besides, I was done covering for him. These bruises were his legacy.

I stepped into the shower and turned it up hot, hoping it might wash away my sins. It didn't. But it did lead me to a few conclusions. I never intended to kill Joe. All I wanted was the chance to leave and start again, but he was never going to let that happen, at least not while there was breath in his lungs. Well, now his lungs were empty, and I was still here.

I turned off the shower and rubbed my hand across the misted glass. My reflection was pink and clean and new. After dressing and pulling my wet hair into a severe ponytail, I emerged from the bathroom to find Frank carrying a second suitcase.

"What are you doing?" I asked nervously.

"Figured if he were going to leave, he'd take some clothes."

I chewed my fingernails and nodded, still unsure whether I should trust him or not.

"If we're going to do this," he said, "it has to be right. Otherwise, we're *both* going to prison."

"Okay."

"Speaking of being right, where's Joe's passport?"

"Why?"

Frank's expression hardened. "I'm getting tired of the questions, but I'll bite this time. He's gonna need to make a trail or questions are gonna get asked. Also, if suspicions do get aroused and the police start asking questions, you're gonna be thankful for that trail. Now stop wasting time and find the passport."

Joe's passport was in the cupboard by the balcony. I opened it and examined his picture for a few seconds. It didn't capture his essence. The eyes were devoid of cruelty, and there was no tension in the face. It could have been anybody but my husband.

"Any other paperwork you'd like me to find while I'm here?" I asked.

Frank ignored the sarcasm in my voice. "Well, since you asked so nicely, I'm figuring you've got a joint account, right?"

"What makes you think that?"

"I've met a lot of men like Joe in my time," he replied. "Every single one was a control freak. And what better way of controlling somebody than by monitoring their money. I'll lay down good odds that you don't even have a bank card, right?"

A blush warmed my cheeks. The bruise beneath my left eye throbbed. My silence spoke volumes because he continued:

"How much is in your account?"

"A few grand — I think."

"Good."

"Why?"

"Because a man answering your husband's description is going to clear the account in the next few days."

"But…"

"Let me finish," Frank interrupted. "Half goes towards paying for his disposal. The rest you'll get in cash from me once all the costs are totted up."

I didn't like it, but I kept my mouth shut. Frank was helping me get rid of my problem, the least I could do was go along with the plan.

"So now what?" I asked.

"Now we get going."

3.

FRANK WAITED at the door until the sound of nearby footsteps began to fade. Then he turned the handle, walked into the dim hallway and dragged the case containing my husband towards the elevator. I followed with the smaller case containing his things and looked around nervously until Frank hissed at me to relax.

I didn't relax, but I tried not to appear quite so shifty.

Frank hit the down button and waited. The elevator seemed to be stuck on the fifth floor. He checked his watch and cursed under his breath. Voices and laughter emanated from above, followed by the click-clack of stilettos on tiles. Finally, the elevator groaned into life.

I pulled at Frank's jacket sleeve. "We're not getting on with other people, are we?"

He looked over his shoulder. "We've got no choice," he said, wiping my brow with his hand. "Now try and act normal."

The lift stopped moving and the door opened with a ping. Two men and three women, all dressed up for the evening, were crammed in the cubicle. There seemed barely enough room for one other person, never mind two people and suitcases. One of the men sneered in our direction and said: "Lift's full, fella. You'll have to wait your turn."

Ignoring him, Frank lifted the case with a slight groan and made a move for the cubicle. The man stepped forward and placed his right hand on Frank's chest. Letting go of the handle, Frank grabbed the man's forefinger and bent it back. The man cried out and moved back to prevent his finger from being broken. Frank matched him step-for-step and pinned him against the cubicle wall. His friends drew away instinctively.

Frank leant in close. "Lay your hands on me again, and the only busy nightspot you'll be visiting is a fucking A&E. Nod if you understand?"

The man nodded once. Frank released his finger and stepped

away. The five friends pressed themselves flat against the back wall, freeing up a surprising amount of space. Frank picked up the case again and stepped inside. I followed him.

The doors closed and the lift trundled into life. The air was hot and stuffy. Every exhalation was as loud as a scream, and every shuffle hurt my eardrums; the tension was so palpable it seemed like an uninvited eighth guest. I wondered if the other occupants heard the rapid pounding of my heart. Sweat rolled down the gulley of my spine and soaked into the waistband of my jeans.

Finally, after a lifetime, the elevator reached the ground floor and the doors separated. Frank lifted the case into the entrance hall and then stepped aside. I did the same. I was too afraid to look at our companions; I didn't want them to see the guilt on my face.

Frank wasn't quite so shy. He turned, smiled, and waved them out of the lift. "Come on then, seeing as though you're in such a hurry."

The group moved past us silently. The man opened the entrance door and held it open for the women and his friend. As soon as they were outside, he turned and stared at Frank. Neither broke eye contact for what seemed like minutes. Finally, the man sneered. "If I see you again, fella, I'm gonna put a fucking knife in your spine."

Frank grinned. "You know Cal Marcus?"

Those four words extinguished the sparkle in the man's eyes. His sneer slipped away. "You don't know him."

"Don't I?"

The man tried to recreate his earlier smirk, but it was a pale photocopy of the original. "What would Cal be doing with an old fucker like you?"

"The same thing as Jack Danning. I'm on good terms with them both."

These names meant nothing to me, but they obviously suggested something to the man holding the door. His tongue darted around his lips repeatedly and nervously. He turned in the direction of the estate.

"Maybe I'll get one of them to pay you a visit," Frank said. "You're on the fifth floor, *right?*"

"Fella..."

"You wanna turn around now, and *fuck* in the general direction of *off*," Frank said, "before I lose what little is left of my temper."

The man shut the door carefully, backed away without breaking eye contact with Frank, then turned on his heels and sprinted away, his arms and legs pumping manically. He gave us one last over the shoulder look before he disappeared behind an adjacent building.

Frank turned to me and said: "Shall we get going?"

I nodded, and we exited the building.

Cold night air stippled my forearms with goosebumps. I grabbed the case and shivered my way through the estate with Frank huffing close behind. Teenage voices hollered abuse in the distance. A scream of anger answered them. Every sound made me twitch and scan the area for danger. By the time we reached my husband's car, I was a sweaty, hyperventilating mess.

I pulled the keys from my pocket and immediately dropped them on the tarmac. Every attempt at retrieval was foiled by shaking hands and fumbling fingers. Frank watched with increasing irritation until he crouched down and scooped them off the ground. Without a word, he unlocked the boot and threw my case inside. It took several big heaves to lift the case containing my husband into the car. Frank was still panting for breath when he climbed into the driver's seat and opened the rear passenger door for me.

This gave me pause for thought, followed by a sharp jolt of fear. "Why the back seat?"

"Because you're going to lie down on it."

My brain conjured all manner of grim scenarios. Fear kept me rooted to the spot. "Why?"

Frank let out an exasperated sigh. "I'm trying to construct a story of your husband leaving you. In that scenario, you do not go for a joyride into London's dirty arsehole with him."

I clambered onto the back seat and curled into the foetal position.

"You said London's arsehole? Whereabouts?"

Frank turned the key. "If I tell you, will you shut up?"

"Maybe."

The engine spluttered into life. "Not far from Tottenham."

"Why?"

"To see a man about a dog."

"Is that code?

"Yes and no."

The car started moving, but there were lots of turns and very few stretches when Frank seemed to put his foot down. The occasional glance out of the window showed houses, flats, and quiet streets.

"Why're we avoiding the main roads?"

"I thought we had a deal?"

"I remember saying maybe."

After a long silence, Frank said: "Main roads have CCTV, most back streets don't. Where possible I wanna avoid cameras. Where I can't avoid cameras, I wanna make sure you can't be seen."

Silence fell once again. Staring at the back of Frank's big head and the detritus in the footwell gave me ample time to think about the situation. Questions bounced around the inside of my skull. Guilt followed in their wake; which brought forth yet more questions. Eventually, there were too many to ask even on a long journey, so I went with the first one that popped into my head.

"Who's Cal Marcus?"

Frank gave me a brief glance in the rear view. "Forget I ever mentioned *him*," he said, before fixing his eyes back on the road.

"That's a little hard to do," I replied. "The fella in the lift turned white when you mentioned his name."

"Then try harder."

"Why?"

"Because mentioning that name in the wrong circumstances is a sure-fire way to get yourself killed."

Fresh goosebumps bubbled to the surface. Just who and what was I mixed up with? More questions popped into my head, but I refrained from asking them in favour of a slightly different topic. "Okay, then. If you won't answer that question, here's another. What do *you* do?"

Frank let out a humourless chuckle. "Don't you ever run out of questions?"

"I've been staring at the back of your head and crushed Coke cans for the last twenty minutes. I'm bored, so humour me."

"I fix things that maybe shouldn't be fixed."

"That means literally nothing."

"For people who don't deserve my help."

The words stung. "D'you mean me?"

"No, I don't mean you," he replied. "I solve people's problems."

"What people?"

"The kind of people you'd cross the road to avoid if you knew what they were capable of."

I tried to ask another question, but Frank ignored it in favour of his phone. "Stevie, I need your help. Why? Because I'm calling in a favour, that's why? I'll cancel that poker debt if you get to Tony's place in the next fifteen minutes. *Why*? Because I need backup. You seem to have more whys than a Welsh place name, my friend, and I'm getting awfully fucking sick of hearing them.

"You know as well as I do that Tony's about as trustworthy as a politician. I need somebody watching my back. Well, look at it another way. If you're *not* at Joe's place in fifteen, I'm gonna sell your debt to Cal. Try telling him some of the bullshit stories you've fobbed me off with. Then you can try telling him again, *after* he's removed your fucking tongue. Okay then, see you in fifteen. Oh, and Stevie, don't forget your metal."

4.

THE CAR came to a halt about twenty minutes later, though the engine continued to hum and sputter. I peered over a window rim at an estate of low-rise hangars in various shades of corrugated macho. Bricks, windows and aesthetically pleasing architecture were few and far between, but they were more than made up for by a proliferation of tall, spiked fences and manly signs in Arial and Helvetica Bold.

A thin figure in a hooded top that cast its face entirely in shadow emerged from the darkness and approached the driver's side of the vehicle. Frank wound down the window.

"Franko," the figure said.

"Stevie."

"I take it there's a good fucking reason for me to be hanging around the shadows like some kinda fucking rent boy?"

"How long've you been here?"

"Long enough for two fellas to drive past and ask if they could borrow my arsehole for ten minutes."

Frank snorted. "Guessing that didn't go well for them?"

Stevie nodded. "Told them to make a beeline for the North Circular before I dragged them from their vehicles and beat seven shades of shit outta them."

Stevie's hood turned in my direction. "Who's the woman?"

"She's nobody."

The hood tipped me a single nod. "Hello, nobody."

"Has anybody visited Tony since you've been here?"

"Saw Minty's van go through the side gate a couple of minutes before you arrived."

Frank exhaled a long, sad sigh. "Thanks, Steve."

"No worries."

"D'you bring some metal?"

Stevie lifted his top. A gun handle poked over the belt of his jeans.

Frank revved the engine. "Give us five minutes before following us in."

"You sure?"

Frank drummed the steering wheel with his fingers. "Tony will wanna play with us a bit."

Play with us? My heart skipped. A cold sweat formed on my brow. I wiped it away with my palms.

Stevie shrugged as he backed away. "Then you better make a trail, if you want me to find you," he said. "It's like a fucking maze in there."

"Just follow the receipts," Frank replied, putting his foot down.

By the time I peered over the rim of the rear window, Stevie had disappeared. I searched the shadows, but there was no movement. Eventually, Frank told me to put my bloody head down.

After another thirty seconds of driving, we came to a building that had no business on an industrial estate. It was a pleasant red brick structure with big windows and a friendly, almost homely appearance that was spoiled only by the high brick walls surrounding the property. The sign above the front door read *A. Scaife & Sons — Veterinary Surgery and Pet Funerals*. I placed my hand over my mouth to smother the laughter, but Frank heard it anyway.

"Sorry we fucked up Fluffy's surgery, Mrs Hammond," Frank said in plummy tones. "But we do offer *excellent* rates on cremations."

The car came to a stop in front of a gate to the left of the main building. Frank looked over his shoulder at me. "Once we're inside, keep schtum. Even by the standards of the average creep, Tony's a *weird* fucking guy. If he thinks you're taking an interest in his business, he's gonna ask you some crazy questions or engage you in some light conspiracy theories. Then, at some point, he's gonna ask you to fuck him or suck him off."

This time the cold sweat prickled along my spine. "I'm not..."

"I *know* that," Frank interrupted. "I just want to make sure *you* know it."

Then he grabbed his phone again and placed a call.

"We're here, Tone," he said. There was a short pause followed by, "Yes, *we*, as in plural... I haven't got time to indulge in your bullshit,

Anthony. Open the fucking gate now before I give you a plural of kicks to the head."

Frank ended the call and put the phone away.

He eyed me in the rear-view.

"Remember, keep schtum."

5.

THE GATE opened on its own. The car moved slowly into a small deserted car park. A quick glance showed no sign of a van, although in a shadowy alcove towards the back of the building there was a van-shaped object covered with a large tarp. Frank gave no indication that he noticed it.

The moment we were both out of the vehicle, a man so large and round he looked like he had his own gravitational system came out of the building to greet us. The white coat wrapped around his frame was about the same size as the tarp covering the van. His small face, which seemed to disappear within a vast expanse of his flabby head, sported a friendly yellow smile. His arms were wide open.

"Franky, my man. Give me a hug," his voice resembled Frank's plummy parody.

"I'll do no such thing."

"What's the matter with you?"

"I just don't fancy getting that close."

The man waved his arm like he was deflecting the insult. "Come on, big fella, there's no hard feelings here." Then his tiny eyes fixed on my face after a slow sweep of my body. "Although if you keep bringing me such exquisite creatures, there'll be some *very* hard feelings, let me tell you."

"Keep your eyes to yourself," Frank warned.

"In the face of such beauty that's quite impossible."

I shrank away until I was partly shielded by Frank, who said: "Then maybe I should keep your eyes in my back pocket. You know, just for safe keeping."

"Now, now, Francis, let's not be nasty."

"Then leave the woman alone."

"Fine, have it your way."

Frank opened the boot and lugged the big case to the ground. "We need to get rid of the contents in a hurry."

The man's gaze stopped lingering on me for long enough to scan the object with disinterest. "Who is it?"

"Nobody you know."

"Then why am *I* disposing of it?"

"Because you can't stop losing at high stakes poker with dangerous people, Tony."

The fat man huffed. "At least tell me it's in pieces."

"Alright then, it's in pieces."

"You know smaller pieces burn faster."

"It happened in a hurry," Frank said. "I didn't have the time for the usual routine."

Tony scowled at Frank. "So I get that onerous task instead?"

"Nice word."

"You like that?"

Frank nodded.

"Thanks. You can find it in the thesaurus beside the synonym burden, which you definitely fucking are."

"Now who's being nasty?"

"Because you're making me nasty."

"Come on, Tone. I'll make it worth your while."

The fat man's eyes narrowed. "How?"

"I'll fix your debt with Cal permanently, and the woman will fix you up with a grand."

"Does she have the cash now?"

"Later."

"How much later?"

"A couple of days max."

A small smile twisted Tony's mouth and his eyes explored my body again. "I know a way she can pay me. A better way."

I started shivering. A small whimper escaped my lips.

"I think cash will do just fine," Frank replied.

"You don't know what I have in mind."

"What you have in mind usually involves anal."

Tony turned away in disgust. "Fine, insult me. I was going to offer to carry the bags, but you can lug them yourself."

He strode off back the way he came.

With a groan, Frank lifted the case and looked at me. "Whatever happens next, be ready for it."

6.

TONY LED us along a labyrinthine series of corridors. He didn't bother glancing back in our direction. If he had, he would have noticed Frank leaving behind a trail of old receipts and tissues from his left trouser pocket as he dragged his case one-handed. Finally, we reached a half-open door to a staircase leading down into the darkness.

Tony pushed through the door and sauntered down the steps. Frank left his wallet outside the door, sent a quick text message, and lugged the case down the stairs. I looked around once and then followed them into the darkness.

We emerged into a cavernous, dimly lit room with a large furnace burning brightly at the far end.

The first thing that struck me was a wall of heat.

The second thing that struck me was the oppressive humidity.

And the third thing that struck me was a fist.

It was a hard blow to the right jaw that sent me staggering to the left of the room, where I collapsed in a heap on the linoleum floor.

Tony turned on his heels and went for Frank. I'd like to say he was fast for a fat lad, but he wasn't, and Frank brushed him aside before he even had the chance to take his first couple of steps. Tony slipped on the floor and ended up on his stomach. He tried groping me, but I managed to wriggle from his grasp.

There was another large man in the room behind us. He was also wearing a white smock and had a shiny bald head. The only real difference between him and Tony was that he was carrying a gun.

"Hands up, Frank," he said.

"Long-time no see, Minty," he replied, raising his hands high. "Where'd you get the toy?"

Minty sneered. "Picked it up in the Hamley's sale."

Frank stepped forward.

Minty jabbed the weapon towards its target and wagged a disapproving finger with his left hand. "Its toy-like appearance is deceptive," he said. "The bullets *will* kill you."

Frank kept his hands high.

Minty jerked his head towards Tony. "You okay, mate?"

The man beside me sat upright. "I'll live, Oliver."

"Which is more than we can say for *these* two," came the reply.

Tony grinned as he staggered to his feet. "Quite."

"You're gonna regret this," Frank said.

Tony's jowls wobbled with a wet slap as he shook his head. "Probably not. And you're not going to live long enough for regrets," he replied, before turning his amused gaze on me. "You, however, are going to have *plenty* of time for repentance before we're finished."

I made myself small against one of the wall units. "Please don't hurt me."

The two fat men laughed.

Tony said: "I promise there'll be a lot more pleasure than pain, my dear."

"But there will be *some* pain, right?" Minty said.

His partner shrugged. "Of course. Otherwise, how will she ever learn to appreciate the pleasure?"

Minty gave me a lusty grin; half his teeth were missing, which made the smile even more menacing.

Then all his teeth were gone, along with most of his head, in an explosion of blood, bone, and brain matter that struck his partner in the face.

Minty's legs buckled, and he fell on the floor.

Tony dropped to his knees with a shriek of shock and pain and scraped pieces of his friend from his face.

Stevie stood at the door holding a smoking automatic in his right hand. In the other was Frank's wallet. "Think you dropped this, sweetheart." The hood was still pulled up over his head, masking his face in shadow.

Frank made a song-and-dance of patting his trousers. "Well, wouldn't you know it, I think you might be right."

Stevie tossed the wallet to Frank, who scooped it out of the air and tucked it in his back pocket.

"What are we gonna do with the fat lad?" he asked.

Frank shrugged. "That's up to him."

The man looked up at them with hope and half of his friend's head on his face. "Whatever you want will get done," he said in a panicky voice. "The fella in the case is *gone*, Oliver is *gone*. Swear to God, I'll do whatever you ask."

Frank smiled. "Were you really going to kill me?"

Tony lifted his arms in a gesture of despair. "You've been threatening me with Cal for the last year," he said. "I'm fucking desperate, mate. I spend most of my days looking over my shoulder."

"This would have been your last job."

"How was I supposed to know," he replied, his voice breaking. "You've been saying it's my last job for *six* months."

"This time I meant it."

Tony's expression was one of sadness. He knew what kind of mess he was in. His gaze drifted towards the gun in Minty's hand.

"Forget it," Stevie said. "You won't even get close."

Tony slumped and sobbed.

Using the wall units, I managed to clamber to my feet. I was still a bit wobbly from the punch, but otherwise I felt okay. Frank smiled at me, then looked at Stevie.

"Take her home, mate."

The tall man's hooded head nodded once.

"And my debt?" he said.

"Consider it repaid."

A surge of rage made me rush for the gun. Tony tried to halt my progress by swinging his big arms in my direction, but he was too slow to stop me. I pried the gun from Minty's hands and evaded Frank's grasp too. Another swell of anger made me spin on my heels and point the deadly end of the gun at Tony. He yelped and fell back on his arse with his hands in front of his face.

There was a metallic taste in my mouth. At first I thought it was fear, then exhilaration, then finally I realised that in all the excitement I'd bitten my tongue and what I could taste was blood. The urge to put bullets in Tony was overwhelming. He was another abuser in a lifetime full of them. My father, my boyfriends, my husband, and now, finally, this fat piece of shit and his friend. A life of being the victim, the object of pity, always afraid of saying or doing the wrong thing. The lowest of the low.

Well, not anymore.

I cocked back the hammer.

Stevie had me in his sights. It was evident that pulling the trigger was a death sentence, but I didn't care. The pleasure of watching Tony squirm and grimace along the floor was too great. The dark stain spreading down the inside leg of his jeans made me grin.

Frank stepped between the fat man and me. He bellowed at Stevie to lower his weapon and then shielded Tony the way someone might protect a loved one. "You don't need to do this," he said.

"Who said anything about need?"

"Okay then, you don't want to do this."

"Are you sure about that?"

He nodded and moved towards me.

"Pretty much," he said. "Tomorrow, you're gonna wake up and feel like shit. That guilt is going to eat your fucking soul. It'll eat you for days, weeks, even months. What you're experiencing right now is anger — years of it. You're glad your husband's dead, right now, because he was a cunt. In the grand scheme of things, he got what was coming. And the fat fuck squirming on the floor is a cunt, too. There's no doubt *he* deserves what's coming. But if you pull that trigger then you're as big a cunt as they are. And tomorrow you'll be sucking down *double* the guilt.

"What you did to your husband was self-defence. It was you or him. Eventually that guilt will ease, because you'll know it's true. But Tony's finished regardless of what *you* do to him. You shoot him — well, that's murder. Try dealing with that if you can."

Frank was right. As much as I wanted to shoot Tony, a small voice beneath the roaring rage told me to let it go.

"You want to know how you win?"

I nodded.

"You live the best fucking life you can. You do all the shit your husband never allowed you to do, all the shit a useless fuck like Tony can *never* do. You make mistakes, you see the world, you break taboos — well, maybe bend them a little — and generally live without apologies. Then, if you're lucky, you might meet the person of your dreams. And if you put down the gun all those things can happen. But *only* if you give me the gun."

Frank held out his hand. Without thinking, I thrust the gun into his palm. He wrapped his fingers around the weapon and breathed a big sigh of relief. Then he stepped away from Tony and pointed at Stevie.

"Take her home, man."

As I was leaving, I turned around.

Frank stared at the gun in his hand. A slight smile turned the edges of his mouth. He wore a relaxed expression of contentment.

"Did you mean all that stuff you said?" I asked.

He stared at me for a moment and nodded. "Yeah, I did. Now go live your life. And watch out for the guilt."

Then I turned away and ran up the stairs.

I never saw Frank again.

7.

A COUPLE of days later a man answering my husband's description and carrying his passport emptied our joint bank account of thirteen grand. I had no idea Joe managed to save that much. I realised most of that money was probably mine.

After another few days had passed, somebody who looked like Joe broke into the flat and tore it apart. All my husband's stuff disappeared, apart from a few knick-knacks, and most of my things were destroyed.

When the police finally responded to my call, I told them about the beatings, and constructed a lie about him trashing the flat in revenge for kicking him out. I even mentioned the empty bank account. They didn't seem particularly bothered about my plight. Aside from a few cursory checks of the place, and an obligatory sweep of the neighbours, they did nothing.

Cleaning the mess gave me a way to dissipate some of the guilt. Frank was right about the remorse — there was lots of it. The first few weeks were especially unpleasant. Nightmares were frequent. Insomnia became my closest friend.

I knocked on Frank's door several times — hoping for words of comfort, or at least a comfortable bed — but he never answered. Eventually, one of his neighbours mentioned that he'd moved out.

For a while, I went from home to work and back again in one continuous cycle of monotony. Conversations were scarce. I performed my job without enthusiasm. Eventually, Susan called me into one of the meeting rooms. The head of HR watched us from the corner and jotted notes on a pad.

They were making redundancies. A quarter of the workforce was due to leave in the next few months. Those who left without fuss would get two weeks tax-free salary for every year of employment and three months salary in lieu of notice. I had six years in the bag, which would give me six months salary in total, plus my holiday pay.

Enough to go travelling. After all, I had no reason to stay now.

Susan said she was sorry, but it was easy to see otherwise because she found it hard to keep the smirk of amusement off her face.

I told her I would be happy to leave at the earliest opportunity.

No time like the present, Susan suggested.

When I arrived home, there was an envelope on the floor. It was too fat to have slid under the door.

I called Frank's name. There was no answer. To be honest, I didn't expect one. The knowledge that he cared enough to visit was sufficient.

I opened the envelope.

It was crammed with fifties and twenties.

And a note.

Start living your life. Here's a little something to get you started. Check tomorrow's paper. A gift from me and Cal Marcus.

It was signed Fx

That night I booked a one-way ticket to Thailand.

The next day I deposited seven grand in the bank, changed the other five grand into dollars and baht, and went for the first in a long list of vaccinations.

The wait for my appointment was interminable. I passed the time with a newspaper. The story Frank mentioned sat in a tiny box at the corner of page seven.

A fire and explosion had destroyed the premises of Anthony Scaife & Sons. The proprietor, Anthony James Scaife, 42, perished in the blaze. The cause was unknown, but the police believed it to be accidental.

I allowed myself a smile because I knew otherwise.

I went to Thailand and lived more in those three months than I had in all my years of marriage. I apologised for nothing — not even the bad stuff.

My guilt about Joe faded. Then one day it disappeared completely. I stopped blaming myself for everything. I was no longer a victim.

My travels took me to Vietnam, Cambodia, Malaysia, India and Australia, where I met a man. We fell in love. We moved in together.

It was bliss.

I forgot about Joe — mostly. I saw glimpses of him in my dreams.

I forgot about Frank completely.

Then my boyfriend mentioned marriage. I told him about my husband, that we were still married, that I wasn't sure where to send the divorce papers. I didn't mention that crazy night, but I did at least tell him about the beatings.

That's when the phone call came.

Your husband's dead, the caller said.

I neglected to mention I already knew that.

An apartment block in Benidorm went up in smoke before it came crashing down to earth in a pile of smoking rubble. It amazed the authorities that only four people died. They were even more amazed when it turned out that three of the victims were British fugitives who'd been on the run for years.

The other victim was Joe. Or somebody lined up as the patsy.

The stuff that wasn't burnt was badly crushed. The stuff that wasn't crushed was badly burnt.

Identification was impossible.

All they had to go on was Joe's passport and a matching blood type.

That was good enough for me.

I told the authorities to cremate the remains. Just to be sure.

Then they told me about his life insurance. A hundred grand.

I was the only beneficiary.

I asked how long ago he'd taken out the insurance.

Over a year, they said.

That was a miracle, I thought, because he's been dead for over two years.

Then I thought about Frank and smiled.

Somehow he'd made this happen. Somehow he was still looking out for me.

The day they paid the insurance into my bank account, I withdrew a hundred dollars and wandered down to the beachfront. Then I found a dingy bar with an eclectic jukebox and a wide selection of English beers. I bought several pints, paid for enough credits to play the entirety of Exile on Main Street, and lifted my first glass in a toast to an imaginary friend.

"Cheers, Frank, you fucking diamond."

SIX SHOOTER

TO THE GRAVE

To The Grave was first published in a different form in the collection *The Greatest Show In Town and other stories* in 2013. It was written during the redrafting stage of *The Gamblers*, along with what became my first Stanton brothers short story, *One-Sixteenth*.

For the most part, I haven't changed the manuscript that much since its original publication. I've added to the degree of desperation in their situation and tightened up some of the language, along with letting some things play out at a less clipped pace.

STEPHEN HEARD a key scraping around in the lock and turned towards the sound. He considered getting off the cushionless sofa, but lacked the strength to actually do it. Familiar footsteps stomped down the carpetless hallway. Then Joe came into the living room. He was pale and out of breath. The only colour on his face was a couple of faint blotches of pink on his cheeks. He leaned against the mouldy wall and took several deep gasps.

"Those fuckin' kids are getting to be a real problem," he said to nobody in particular.

Stephen scratched the crook of his left forearm nervously. "Please tell me you got the shit?"

Joe eyed him with some irritation. "That's charming, that is," he said. "No *I hope you're okay, mate*, or any concern for my well being. Just straight down to business. Some fuckin' mate you are."

"I'm sorry, man, but I'm running on fumes here. Have you got the shit?"

Joe waved two baggies. "Yeah. I got it."

Stephen gave a sigh of relief. "Thank fuck." He ran a jittery hand across his head to wipe away the beads of junk sweat that were forming on his hairless scalp. The shaved head made him look like a science class skeleton; an effect enhanced by his undernourished physique. His pallid skin was blotchy and mottled and there were old bruises on both of his cadaverous cheekbones. He had bags under his eyes that were large enough to carry groceries.

"What are friends for, right?" Joe said. He looked healthier than his friend, but his once tight frame was getting soft and doughy. Once upon a time he'd been such a regular at the gym that his girlfriend used to tease him about it. She often joked that he loved the gym more than her. When Joe wasn't high he often thought about Jemma. Which was probably why he got high so often.

"Right," Stephen said, his movements twitchy. "I was getting worried for a second."

There was a look of disgust on Joe's face. "Are you for *real*? You thought I'd cut out on you? For fuck's sake."

Stephen shrugged and tried to smile, but it came off as sly. "Nah. It's not that I don't trust you or nowt, but it *is* the last of my money."

"The last of *our* money," Joe said, throwing one of the baggies.

Stephen caught it. "Right. Last of our money."

"So we better make sure this lasts."

Stephen opened the baggie and grinned. "You're a real mate."

Joe shrugged, looking a little embarrassed. "De nada."

"Best friends for life," Stephen said, lifting a can of beer in celebration.

Joe blushed momentarily, then bumped an imaginary tin against the one in his friend's hand and made a clunking noise in acknowledgment. "And to the grave."

Both men took swigs – one real and one imaginary.

Joe looked around the damp squat and suppressed his tears. From a comfortable home to this hell in less than six weeks. The thought of what he'd given up to be here made him want to scream. He stomped around as a distraction from the grief that was tearing at his guts, taking care to avoid the floorboards that were warped with rain water and piss. The corpse of a dead rat decomposed in a darkened corner. Despite the cloying stench, neither man cared enough to actually pick it up and throw it away. Given a choice, they would have chosen anywhere but this, but they were all out of options. It was this hovel or the streets.

"Was Oggie radged?"

"No more than usual."

"Did he say owt?"

"Only that he still wants his money from you."

"He was okay with you, though?"

"I'm here, aren't I? Told him it was *my* cash, so he gave up the shit, but he said you better have his money by the end of the week. Or else."

"Or else what?"

Joe shrugged. "That part he left open. Let your imagination fill the gap, or summat."

"Where are we gonna find more money?"

Joe shook his head. "Fuck knows."

Stephen paused, bit his bottom lip nervously. "I'm sorry, mate."

"Don't worry about it."

"I'm sorry about *all* of it."

Joe's jaw muscles twitched. "It's history."

"I *mean* it," Stephen said, his eyes glistening with tears.

Joe didn't want to talk about the events that ended with him being kicked out by his furious girlfriend. Thinking about it all again made his guts churn and his heart ache. He held back his tears and shook his head in a vain attempt to send the conversation in a different direction. "I don't wanna rake over old coals. I can't change the past."

"But…"

"I'm serious, man. Shut the fuck up."

Remembering all the moments that destroyed his relationship was too much to bear, but Joe did it anyway, running them through his head on a continuous, torturous loop. It started with the lies he told his girlfriend to get Stephen a few nights on their sofa. Further fibs were deployed to extend his stay. These were followed by a series of increasingly elaborate porkies to explain why there was money missing from her purse. The last straw came when Stephen managed to get into Jemma's bank account and steal a couple of hundred quid that went on heroin and hookers. The last image that tumbled through Joe's head was his girlfriend screaming into his face that it was over as she threw his books and clothes into the street.

Stephen gave his baggie a long glance and tapped it with his finger, dispersing the contents. "I didn't think Jemma'd kick you out cozza me."

"We'd been on the edge for a while," Joe replied, while neglecting to mention that it was his friendship with Stephen that had taken them to the edge in the first place. But it had been that way since childhood, with Joe spending most of his time finding ways to get his friend out of trouble. With school mates, with teachers, with the authorities and work colleagues. Trouble followed Stephen even when he tried to stay on the straight and narrow, which was probably why he strayed from the path so often.

"She could still take you back," Stephen said.

Joe shook his head. He sat down on the floor and gave his baggie a quick shake. "It's been over a month, mate."

"She loves you."

"Mebbe she did once. But that was long before we broke up," Joe said with a sigh. Before Jemma had slammed the door in his face, she screamed that she hated him. Her words had sliced him to the bone, but it was the anger in her voice that carved deep into his marrow. Jemma had meant everything she'd said.

"It's not too late."

Joe hung his head momentarily. "A month's a long time," he said with a sharp edge that suggested this topic of conversation was over.

"All I do is bring you down."

Joe looked at Stephen for a long time, then glanced at the baggie in his hand. "Forget it."

"Even when we were kids you stuck up for us."

"Somebody had to."

"Didn't hafta be you."

"You know me. I was always a bit of a touch for a sob story, stray animals, crying women, friends in need. It always takes summat major to cut the ties, know what I mean?"

"Well, it means a lot. You're a quality bloke, mate."

Joe gave him a hard stare. "Can you just fuckin' leave it."

Stephen glanced down at the floor. "Sorry, mate."

"And stop saying sorry, for fuck's sake. It's getting right on my tits."

Stephen went to say something, then checked himself. He gazed at the baggie in his hand and smiled. "Can I have the first taste?"

Joe paused, then shrugged. "Go for it."

Stephen put some of the powder in a spoon, then added some powdered vitamin C. He took a syringe, punctured a plastic bottle of water, drew in the amount he needed, pulled out the syringe and squirted this over the drugs. He mixed everything together with the syringe, cleaned the tip and started heating the underside of the spoon with a lighter. Once he was happy, Stephen dropped a ragged cigarette filter into the liquid and used this to filter the solution into the syringe. Then he tapped the thing several times and brought the air bubbles to the top. A quick squeeze of the plunger released the air and sent a drop of liquid rolling down the needle. Stephen tied a tourniquet around his arm and looked for a healthy vein. There weren't many, but he eventually managed to find something that seemed usable. Then he pushed in the needle and depressed the plunger.

Stephen's initial reaction was to breathe deeply, almost orgasmically, but this was followed by another rapid inhalation. His eyes widened. His fingers drew into tight fists. He slouched back, but then continued to slide to the right until he came to rest with the side of his face pressed against the sofa. Tears rolled down his cheeks and his breathing became ever more shallow.

Joe crouched close to his friend and gave him an affectionate pat on the shoulder. As Stephen's eyes began to take on the glassiness of death, Joe brushed a gentle hand across the man's head and then squeezed the baggie in his hand. "Sorry, mate. It was fifty-fifty. I never could cut my ties, could I? It was always gonna need summat drastic. And, well, this is as drastic as it gets. If it makes it any easier it could've been either one of us, you know. I didn't know which one had the dose. I couldn't leave with you around, mate. I just didn't have the willpower. I'm sorry it ended like this."

When Joe finished talking, he realised he was chatting with a corpse. For the first time in a long time, Stephen looked at peace. The glassy-eyed stare made him seem like he was contemplating something beyond human understanding. Joe envied his friend for a brief moment, until he remembered that he was staring at a corpse.

Deep in thought, Joe rubbed his chin and stared at the poisoned baggie. He rummaged in his pocket until he found an old till receipt and laid it flat in the palm of his hand. He picked up the baggie, poured some of its contents onto the piece of paper, and put it back where he found it. Then Joe folded the receipt carefully and put it back in his pocket.

He smiled at Stephen. "Just in case I can't convince Jemma to take me back."

Joe gave his friend one final pat on the head. Then he stood up and took a last look around the room. Gradually, he drifted into the hallway and walked to the door. He grabbed the handle and held it for a few seconds. A flutter of remorse made his guts quiver. Joe banished the thought by telling himself that it could have gone either way. Then he opened the door, basked in the warm sunlight for a moment, and shuffled away from the scene of the crime.

SIX SHOOTER

THE ACCIDENT

The Accident was first published on a previous blog back in 2015. It hasn't changed much in that time. I have added and subtracted a few words here and there, but this is the one story in this collection that hasn't received a thorough spit and polish.

It's also the closest I've come to a genuine piece of flash fiction. I tend to write long, even when I'm trying to make things short and to the point. *A Man Called Mary* is a prime example of this, but that's only because I loved the characters so much. I really didn't want my time with them to end.

JOHN LOOKED up from beneath the car and said: "Christ, Rog, did you do this intentionally?"

"What makes you say that?" Roger asked.

John shook his head and ducked back under. "Because there's a lotta fuckin' damage here," he replied, his voice slightly muffled by the vehicle that covered him. "And it's not like you're an idiot, mate. So when I see summat that's this level of fucked — well, I've gotta ask."

Roger sighed softly. "It was a bit stupid of me."

"You can say that again."

Roger did a circuit of the jacked-up car, looking at the flat tires and the scratched-up bumpers. It didn't look good from this angle. "Prognosis?"

John cleared his throat. "Back bumper's hanging by a thread. You've put a hole in the exhaust and *that's* barely hanging, and you've somehow fucked three of the tires so they're flat. And then you drove home on the things, so the rims are fucked along with the tires."

"Can you fix it?"

John scoffed. "This is a garage job, mate. I don't have the tools or the time to fix it. Frankly I feel under-qualified just *looking* at it. And I'm only doing it as a favour to you."

"Fair enough," Roger said, as he did a second circuit of the car. "I went over one of those low roundabouts. Not low enough, I guess."

"Don't sound like you."

"I was thinking about other stuff."

"Such as."

"Trouble at home."

John paused momentarily. "Still bad?"

"It's got worse."

John poked his head out from under the car again. "Worse?"

"Yeah."

"Shit," he said, looking uncomfortable. "Is there owt I can do?"

"No more than you've done already."

"Huh?"

"Can you fix marriages and cars?"

John went back beneath the vehicle. "Marriages? You're having a laugh, arent you? If you wanna talk about summat that's unfixable, mate — you might wanna have a peek at my shitstorm of a marriage sometime."

Roger paused. "At least your Missus isn't having an affair."

"An affair? Shit, mate. A... Are... are you sure?"

"I'm sure."

He crouched and looked at the top of his friend's head. "That's why I pranged the car."

John tilted his neck to get a better view of Roger. "Shit, mate. Sorry," he said. "I guess summat like that would make anybody lose control."

"I didn't lose control."

"But, you said..."

"I said it was a bit stupid of me."

John looked at something directly above him and tinkered with it. "Expensive way of venting steam," he said.

"I wasn't venting steam."

John angled his head back at Roger. "So you've inflicted all this damage for no reason?"

"No. I had a reason."

John pulled at a piece of metal and threw it to one side. "Which was?"

Roger took a mobile phone from his pocket and prodded the screen. "I wanted you to look at the car."

John thought about that. "I don't understand."

He got on his knees and crept forward. "This should explain it."

His friend reached out from beneath the vehicle and Roger put the phone in his outstretched hand. He stood up and brushed the knees of his jeans.

The man looked at the text and tried to speak. But he could only stutter.

"Actually, I wanted you *beneath* it."

Now John found his voice. He let out a rapid stream of incomprehensible words. Then he hooked both hands around the base of the vehicle in a frantic attempt to pull himself free.

Roger kicked the jack away. The car seemed to hang in the air. For a split-second, he worried that it wasn't going to fall at all, and that, somehow, gravity didn't operate normally in his friend's workshop. John continued wriggling and screaming for what seemed an eternity. Finally, the vehicle slammed into the ground. There was a final brief squeal of pain as the life was crushed from him. Two unmoving hands poked out from beneath the hatchback. The mobile lay on its back next to Roger's right thumb. The message on the screen read: *I wanna fuck you tonight, babe. Good and hard. Like you like it. Annie's gone to see her Mum. Make an excuse for Roger. Bring the lingerie I like. John. Xxx*

Roger squatted on his haunches for a view of the corpse. He saw a strip of bloodied hair in the light, but the rest was in shadow. It was good enough.

He smiled, stood and left the garage. He closed the door behind him.

MARTIN STANLEY

SIX SHOOTER

YOU'RE WORTH MORE THAN YOU THINK

You're Worth More Than You Think was first published in *The Greatest Show in Town*. It's tied with *The Carpenter's Arms* as being my favourite piece from that collection (including the Stanton brothers' tales). But when I re-read it recently, I felt that it could do with some changes to make it really sing. Some tightening of the language was needed at the beginning of the tale, along with more detail about the protagonist's predicament.

There are fewer language tweaks during the latter half of the tale, but the things I did change help make things clearer for readers and remove any muddy sentences and imprecise language.

JOHN PINKNEY sat on the sofa and smirked. It was the cocky smile of a man whose father was worth a fortune in old money. A man who, despite all evidence to the contrary, believed that the family estate would one day fall into his lap.

Pinkney's terrible life choices had ruined that possibility. All lines of family credit had been exhausted over the last decade, and he hadn't spoken to his father in nearly half that time. He'd been chased out of every family home at one point or another, until his only options were junky hovels or the streets, and yet, despite all of this, he still believed that if he cleaned up his act, dear Daddy would invite him back into the fold and forgive all his indiscretions.

The people addicts lie to most are themselves.

He ran a hand through his greasy blonde hair and flashed his teeth. Pinkney still thought his smile worked, that it hadn't been ruined by bad living and weeks on end without a toothbrush. Whenever he looked in a mirror, Pinkney ignored his rotten teeth and pallid, spot-encrusted skin because any acknowledgement would confirm how bad things were. And he especially ignored his ill-fitting clothes, because many of them still carried the logos that showed how expensive they were when he bought them many years ago.

"Why're *you* smiling?" asked Mike Bennett.

"Because I'm worth something to you."

Now it was Mike's turn to smile, which caused creases to form in his wood-hued face. Too many hours on the sunbed, and thirty years of smoking, made the man look far older than his forty-five years. He rummaged through a jacket pocket for a cigarette and lighter. He placed the cancer stick in his mouth, took a drag, and watched Pinkney with cold blue eyes. While his cigarette burned, he said nothing. He observed the posh boy like he was a specimen on a slide. Then he stubbed out the fag and broke the silence. "Get this through your thick skull. You're worth *nothing* to me. In fact, I need you like I need a second arsehole. To be honest, if I could get somebody, any-fucking-body, that wasn't you to do it, I would. But I've used up my supply of idiots, which leaves me with the fucking morons. And as you're number one in that select group, I figured you might wanna make some cash. But if you're gonna be a prick about it…."

Pinkney's grin changed from arrogant to obsequious in the twitch of a few facial muscles. Mike told him to stop smiling. He did as he was told.

"Do you wanna make some money, or not?"

"I need the cash, mate."

"I'm not your mate," Mike replied. "I'm your boss. You should remember that."

Pinkney nodded.

"D'you fancy a trip to Northumberland?"

"What's in Northumberland?"

"None of your beeswax."

"So why am I going?"

"To meet a contact."

"I assume you're not gonna tell me who?"

"For once, you've assumed correctly."

"Why the secrecy?"

"Coz I told my contact that I'd keep shit on a need to know basis. And right at this moment, you don't need to know"

Pinkney worked at his fingernails the way a terrier works a toy, shaking his head as he tore at them. "Is there *anything* you can tell me?"

"You're gonna be a mule."

"What am I gonna be hauling?"

"You can discuss all that shit with my contact when you meet him."

Pinkney considered asking further questions, but thought better of it. The atmosphere in the room was already dreadful, and every time he opened his mouth it only made things worse. Pinkney needed the work and the money, and he wouldn't be getting either if he pissed off his boss so badly that he kicked him out of the office. So he kept the questions to himself. The cash he needed to feed his habit was more important.

That fleeting thought reminded him of something: he needed a fix.

It had been several hours since his last hit and he was surviving on its last fumes. His hands had been shaking for at least half an hour. To disguise the condition, Pinkney had clasped both hands together tightly, until his knuckles blanched, and pressed them into his lap.

Despite the pretence, Mike noticed his desperation. "You look like you need a fix."

Pinkney tried to smile, but realised that it was more of a grimace. "I'm fine. Good to do whatever it is you need me to do."

Besides, he had a baggie at home. There was enough in it for a couple of shots. He'd pick it up on the way to Northumberland, or wherever the fuck it was that his boss was sending him.

Mike leaned forward and his eyes narrowed. "Did you tell anybody we were meeting today?"

Although he loved to brag, Pinkney had kept his mouth shut. For once, his desire to make money outweighed his need to bluster. Nobody knew he was here. Even so, he couldn't help but blush as he protested his innocence. "What do you take me for?"

"A fucking idiot," Mike replied, "but that doesn't answer my question."

Pinkney held up his hands and pulled a face that seemed to say, *fair enough*. "I haven't said a thing to anyone. I'm being straight with you."

Mike let out a soft chuckle laced with menace.

"A fuckin' spirit-level couldn't get you straight, lad."

Pinkney sighed. "Seriously, if I'm such a twat, why're you sending me outta town?"

"*Because* you're a twat, that's why. You're bloody useless at everything I've asked you to do over the years, but this is summat even you should be able to manage. And before you ask, it's a new business venture. There's money in it for the right people, and there's money in *you*, lad. Even you can't fuck it up, I think."

Pinkney shaped up to say something, but Mike cut him off. "Take it up with my partner when you see him."

"When will I see him?"

"No time like the present?"

"Now, you mean?"

Mike rolled his eyes. "No. Sixty years in the future, you cunt. Yes, fuckin' now."

"Well…"

"Well, what?"

"I'm not ready."

"Sure you are."

"I need to gather some things."

"Such as?"

Pinkney shrugged and thought about the baggie at home. A fleeting flicker of guilt darkened his face and he coughed. "Travel provisions."

"Who the fuck d'you think you are? Phileas Fogg? You're not going around the world, you silly twat."

"What about clothes and things like that? I'll need toiletries if I'm gonna be away for a bit."

Mike flicked the wheel of the Zippo lighter a few times. The sparks jumped without lighting a flame. He only played with it when he was angry. "What you really mean is you need enough smack to get you through a three hour journey."

Realising that he was on the verge of talking his way out the money, Pinkney shut his mouth and waited, his jaw clenching and unclenching, his fingers clutching at the hem of his t-shirt, stretching the fabric almost to ripping point before he let go.

Now it was Mike's turn to smirk.

"You go *now*, or you don't go at all. My contact will sort you out when you arrive, okay?"

Pinkney dipped his head slightly and mumbled in agreement.

"There's a car waiting outside. Now, get out."

Pinkney left the office, walked through the vacant bar area and out of the building. Once outside, he took a huge gulp of air and realised that he was drenched with sweat. His sticky t-shirt clung to his body and his jeans were wet to the touch. Pinkney rummaged with his clothes for a bit and pulled damp underwear from his arse crack. After a few pointless seconds of wafting his t-shirt around in an attempt to cool himself down, the junky looked around for his ride.

There was a gleaming black BMW four-door parked across the street. The engine purred softly. It wasn't Mike's usual type of car — he was more of a pimped-out Rover kind of guy — but Pinkney wasn't going to complain about travelling in style. He crossed the road and leaned towards the front passenger, but stopped himself.

He'd expected to see Mike's usual driver, Denny Morris, in the front seat, but the stranger who turned in his direction looked more like a bouncer than a wheelman. His big face was as stoic as an Easter Island statue. Mirrored shades covered his eyes and made him appear inscrutable. He tipped the merest hint of a nod in Pinkney's direction.

"Are you my pick-up?" he asked. The voice and the face didn't fit. Pinkney had expected the rough rasp of a man who gargles with gravel. Instead, the driver spoke with a soft, unaccented voice. "Yes? No?"

"Yeah."

"Then let's not waste time, sir. We should get going."

Pinkney looked closer at the man. His arms stretched the fabric of his suit, making it look like a second, shinier skin, and his hands were the size of baseball gloves. The driver had pushed his seat back as far as it could go, yet he still seemed to fill every available inch of space.

Something about the situation didn't feel right. The driver put him on edge, even though he wasn't sure why. His internal voice, the one that valued self-preservation above all else, told him that the driver wasn't what he appeared to be. Pinkney hesitated and considered walking away. Then the other voice kicked in, the one that told him heroin was a good idea, and that he didn't need his father's help, reminded him how much he needed the money.

"Are you getting in, sir?"

Pinkney opened the rear door and climbed inside. The sweet scent of soft leather filled his nostrils and reminded him of childhood drives with his father. An air-conditioned breeze caressed him and started working its magic on his damp clothes. Classical music drifted out of the stereo. He didn't recognise the composer, but the music soothed him. He felt more relaxed, and momentarily forgot that he didn't trust the driver.

"Are you one of Mike's usual crew?"

The driver angled his head towards the rear-view mirror. Shades or no shades, Pinkney could tell that he was looking at him.

"Who?"

"Then you're working for the other fella."

"What other fellow?"

"The guy we're going to see."

"*We're* not going to see anybody," the man said, his voice emotionless. "*I'm* just taking you from A-to-B. What you do when you get there is your business."

"Well, *somebody* hired you?"

The man turned in his seat and faced Pinkney.

"This journey will go better if you fasten yourself in," he said.

"Look, I'm just asking you a question."

The man smiled for the first time. His sharp white teeth gave him a lupine, ferocious look, like he was baring his fangs in readiness for an attack. His expression heightened Pinkney's sense of dread.

"I can't answer what I don't know, sir," he replied. "I was told to pick up a passenger, but wasn't told who. I was told what the drop-off point would be and that's all. If I could tell you more, I would. It seems that we're both in the dark on this one."

Pinkney gave him a smile and wiped sweat off his top lip. "Sorry. I'm just a bit nervous."

"I can tell."

"This all feels really weird."

The driver nodded. "Then leave. There's nothing stopping you, sir. I get paid either way."

Pinkney looked out of the window at the sun drenched concrete architecture. Heat haze shimmered up from the pavements. In the distance, beyond the roofs, smoke stacks pumped pollution into the sky. Pinkney shivered and thought of every reason why he should get out of the car and never look back. Dozens came to mind but none was as powerful as his reason to stay – he always needed money for his next fix.

"No. Let's go," he said.

"Then buckle up, sir," the driver said. "It's a long drive."

Pinkney made several attempts at conversation but gave up when he realised the driver wasn't interested. He asked the man to turn up the music to cover the uncomfortable silence. Golden fields of rape blurred into green pastures that began to rise until they became tree peppered hill ranges. Pinkney felt the warm sun on his face and chest and his eyelids began to droop. He tried to fight it at first, jerking upright whenever his chin hit his chest, but gradually he stopped struggling and let himself fall asleep.

Pinkney jerked upright, looked around in confusion, and remembered where he was. He rubbed his eyes and looked out of the window. The car sat in front of a sprawling sandstone farmhouse that encompassed numerous ugly extensions and ramshackle barns. Aware that he was being watched, Pinkney turned back towards the driver.

"This us?"

"According to the satnav."

"How long have we been parked?"

"You woke the second I came to a stop, sir."

Pinkney gave the farmhouse another look and wondered why nobody had come out to greet him. A moment of disappointment was tempered with the knowledge that nobody ever respects a mule. Bitter experience had taught him that fact. All your humanity goes out of the window once you swallow a junk-filled condom or stick it up your arse. You become a possession to be pushed and prodded from pillar to post.

He sighed and asked: "Are you coming in?"

The driver shook his head. "My job's done, sir. I'm going home now."

Pinkney pushed aside his unease and exited the vehicle. There was a cloying stench of hay and manure in the warm air. Pinkney held his breath and walked towards the house. The BMW started its engine, reversed out of its parking spot, and drove away. Pinkney slowed and watched it disappear behind a thicket of tall trees.

He was alone now.

He knocked on the front door and waited. He was tempted to turn the handle and enter, but he wanted to make a good impression. So he waited. After several minutes and several more knocks, there was the clack of hard soles on tiled flooring.

The door opened, and a tall man in a well-fitted suit with neat grey hair gave him the once over. He smiled with his mouth, but his eyes were as blank and dark as a freshly cleaned blackboard.

"You must be John."

"That's me."

"You should have come in."

"I didn't think it would be appropriate."

The man's smile widened. "We don't stand on ceremony here."

He stepped back and gave him room to enter, but Pinkney didn't move. Despite his fear, and the craving for junk that gnawed at him, he believed he deserved some answers. "Well *I* do. I'd also like to be told why I'm here?"

"Didn't Mike say?"

"He kept his cards close to his chest."

"We asked him to send us somebody useful."

"He said I was *useful*?"

"Of course. You wouldn't be here otherwise."

Over the years, Mike had never given Pinkney the credit he felt he deserved. Instead, he mocked him relentlessly and called him every filthy name under the sun. But now a man he'd never met before had spoken to him with respect and told him that Mike considered him valuable. This changed things for Pinkney. He walked inside.

The man guided him into a large living room, where he was struck by an overpowering wall of heat. A wood burning fire raged beneath a chimney column that took up most of the far wall. His skin flushed and sweat rolled down his back. Pinkney wiped his brow and took in his surroundings.

A thin, bald man with prominent cheekbones and deep-set eyes read a magazine on a sofa beside the fire. The man looked up, tossed his reading material aside, and gestured at his guest to sit. Pinkney found a nearby armchair and sank into it.

The thin man looked at his associate. "Geoffrey, fix our friend a drink."

"Of course, what would you like, John?"

"Just a mineral water if you've got it," Pinkney said and paused. "Because, you know, I'm feeling thirsty after the drive."

"No need to explain," the thin man said. "Travel is hard on the body. Anyway, you can have a proper drink later, if you like."

Geoffrey wandered out of the room. The thin man sat forward with his elbows on his knees and his hands clasped and gave Pinkney his full attention.

"Presumably you've got questions."

Pinkney nodded. "Why am I here? Geoffrey said Mike considered me... *useful*?"

The man smiled. "You sound surprised."

"My boss seems to think I'm a cu... a, er... not much cop generally."

"A couple of weeks ago he made you take some blood tests, right?"

Pinkney narrowed his eyes and nodded slightly. "Yeah. You know about that? He said something about wanting a clean organisation. Everybody thought he'd gone crazy or something. We all had to take the tests. Some guys really shi… a, er… really got worried about that. Hell, they took blood samples, urine samples, the whole shebang. They even made us run."

"That was for our benefit."

"I don't get it."

"You aren't supposed to."

"Then, why?"

"We were looking for a specific person for our new business venture, somebody healthy."

"To be a mule?"

The man smiled again. "Of a sort."

Geoffrey wandered back into the room and handed Pinkney a glass of water. He drained it in a couple of swigs and set it down on the table. "Not being funny, mate, but most of the mules I know are smackheads."

"Like you."

"I'm not…"

The thin man smiled. "An addict? That's not what your blood samples told us."

Pinkney's face burned, though it wasn't the heat causing it this time. "I suppose I didn't think about that."

"Most people don't. They don't think about the numerous indiscretions that blood and urine samples reveal. In fact, I'm surprised you're as healthy as you are. No HIV, no hepatitis, no sexually transmitted diseases and internally you seem to be functioning just fine."

Pinkney didn't feel healthy. His stomach lurched. He felt sick, but fought the sensation because he didn't want to look any worse in front of this man. His cravings for heroin had brought on similar effects in the past, though never as strong and never as fast.

The sickness passed and was replaced by a feeling he knew well. Everything was soft and hazy, like the world was smothered within a cotton wool hug. Heroin gave him a similar feeling. Pinkney looked at the glass of water and realised he'd been spiked. Because it was so hot, he'd downed it without thinking. He tried to get out of the chair, but his legs were rubbery and unable to support his weight. Pinkney collapsed back in his seat and tried to look at the thin man, but his eyes had lost all focus.

"How are you doing there?" the thin man asked.

Pinkney tried to speak, but his tongue felt as fat and useless as a bloated slug. His words emerged as a mangled jumble of consonants. The thin man shook his head and told him to say it again.

"You... spiked m... m... me."

"That's right."

Pinkney tried to stand up again, but his legs didn't respond. He slumped back in his chair. Even though there was no point in struggling, he couldn't help but try to get out of the seat one more time.

"Don't fight it. You'll only make it worse if you do."

Pinkney stopped fighting, closed his eyes, and was unconscious before he had the chance to draw another breath.

A red shimmer was the first thing he noticed, followed by a sensation of heat. It took him some time to adjust, but Pinkney gradually realised that it was simply bright light filtering in through his eyelids. He opened his eyes and whimpered in pain. The strong glare almost burned out his retinas. He blinked and turned his head away. For several seconds the silhouette of the retinal burn obscured his vision. It changed from dark blue to a transparent red, before finally disappearing completely.

In front of him were several large plastic containers with handles. They resembled the cold boxes his ex-girlfriend used for picnics, back in the days before his addiction. Standing in front of them was a man in a white scrubs, white gloves, a cap, and a mask covering the lower half of his face. It looked like Geoffrey, but Pinkney was too spaced out to be sure. There was another man beside him, a stocky giant dressed in identical surgical gear. Pinkney was certain that this was the driver. His unpleasant, deep-set eyes stared at something Pinkney couldn't quite see.

He followed the giant's gaze and noticed the thin man looking down at him with some irritation. He was dressed like his associates. The only difference was the blood-stained scalpel in his hand. The man looked up at Geoffrey.

"You didn't drug him properly."

"I *did* drug him properly."

"Then why is he awake?"

"Probably because he's a junky. I guess he needs a stronger dose."

"Get the chloroform."

Pinkney tried to move but couldn't. He shifted his head from side-to-side and realised his hands were strapped to the gurney. Attempting to kick out with his legs had the same result, which meant they were also secured.

He lifted his head and angled his eyes until he reached his exposed torso. A red slash had been cut into the top of his belly, just below the start of his ribcage. Blood oozed from the cut. Pinkney attempted to lift his head again, but try as he might he was unable to see where the cut ended. He began hyperventilating, panicking.

The thin man sighed and rolled his eyes. "Geoff, you might want to hurry it up with that."

"What's going on?" said Pinkney.

"Shush now."

"What. Is. Going. On?"

"*Geoff?*"

"What. Are. You. Putting. In. Me?"

The thin man stopped momentarily and the corners of his eyes crinkled, then creased. He let out a soft chuckle.

"Not too bright, are we?"

"What? But I'm a mule."

"Oh, yes, that's right."

"Then..."

"Of a sort, I believe I said."

"I don't..."

"Understand? You've been carrying what we wanted around with you all this time."

"Is there something inside me?"

The man's eyes creased again. "Quite a lot, actually."

Pinkney tried to think of a time when Mike could have put something inside him without his knowledge. He couldn't think of a specific occasion, though he knew that there were many times it could have happened. Drug induced narcolepsy was a common problem for him. Still, he didn't have any scars. So how was it possible?

"Something slipped inside me?"

"You really are an idiot, aren't you?"

"I don't..."

"Organs, Mr Pinkney."

Geoffrey came back into the room and moved towards the trolley. He had a small brown bottle in one hand and a rag in the other.

Pinkney realised what was happening, what Mike had planned all along. Pinkney told himself he didn't deserve what was happening, but knew in his heart that this wasn't the case. It was obvious that pleas weren't going to work with these people but he tried them anyway.

"People'll miss me."

"No they won't."

Geoffrey unscrewed the bottle.

"My father…"

"Wrote you off a long time ago."

Geoffrey poured the liquid into the cloth. Its stench filled the room. The thin man leaned over Pinkney.

"Your girlfriend is dead. Overdose, I believe. You probably gave her the final hit, though nobody could prove it. You haven't had a bank account or a job in years. You've never been on an electoral register. You have no fixed abode. Your boss sure as hell won't miss you. As far as the system is concerned you're already gone. This will only seal the deal."

"Please. Don't do this."

Geoffrey moved in close. Pinkney could barely breathe through the reek of the chloroform. The thin man looked into his eyes.

"It's already done. We've been selling you to the highest bidder for the past fortnight. Your kidneys are worth thirty grand each, did you know that? No, I don't suppose you did. Your lungs are worth fifty apiece. Your heart's worth a hundred grand to a wealthy businessman in China and your liver's going to an alcoholic Russian oligarch for pretty much the same. Your corneas will fetch twenty. You're worth more than you think, Mr Pinkney."

He struggled until the table straps bit deep into his flesh, until they drew blood.

The man's eyes creased again. "But, of course, that's not going to do you much good."

Geoffrey put the cloth over his face. Pinkney held his breath for as long as he could, but it wasn't long enough. He shook his head and tried to gasp around the rag, but the thin man's helper had a firm grasp on him. He took in a mouthful of fumes and started going under. As he faded out, Pinkney thought about summer drives with his father, with the wind blowing his hair when the soft top came down.

Then he was gone.

SIX SHOOTER

THE CARPENTER'S ARMS

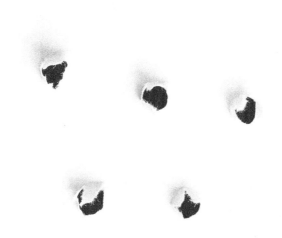

The Carpenter's Arms was first published in *The Greatest Show in Town*. In some respects I consider it to be the flipside of *You're Worth More Than You Think*. Whereas Pinkney is a terrible human being whose fate is brought about by a lifetime of dreadful choices, Stephen Cresswell is a decent man whose foolish decision puts him in the worst situation. My recent redraft changed some things I wasn't happy with in the original version, mostly to do with his wife, who's a screaming one-note harpy in the the 2013 incarnation. In this version she's a good woman trying to do right by her family. The story is all the better for it. Along with this are some revisions of language to make things smoother and tighter for the reader.

This is honestly one of my favourite things that I've written.
I really hope you enjoy it.

1.

STEPHEN STARED at the dregs of cheap whisky at the bottom of his plastic shot glass and thought about buying another. He drained the last drops and placed the glass on the countertop. His gaze was drawn to the small selection of spirit bottles on the wall opposite.

There were two Scottish whiskies that tasted antiseptic, a knock-off Irish with the name *Jamison* rather than *Jameson*, and there was a bottle of amber liquid called *Kentucky Rye*. The rest of the display consisted of no-brand bottles of gin, vodka, and brandy. The Carpenter's Arms wasn't renowned for its drinks.

"You've been staring at the wall for five minutes," the landlord said. "Those whiskies you've been slamming are as good as it gets in here. Maybe you should think about calling it a night."

The landlord was wary because he'd just watched him put away four doubles in the space of twenty minutes. Normally, this much booze on an empty stomach would have been enough to put Stephen on his back. But these weren't normal circumstances. The adrenaline jack-knifing through his veins was keeping him sober. Sweat ran down his back and collected in the crack of his arse. The sensation was unpleasant enough to make Stephen shuffle around on the creaky barstool.

"I'm not ready to call it a night, mate. Gimme a double Kentucky."

The short, stocky man grinned without amusement. He glowered at Stephen with mean blue eyes and then dumped a couple of measures in a new glass. He slammed the drink down on the counter and put out his hand. Stephen pressed a crumpled note into his palm and told him to keep the change.

This made the landlord crack a genuine smile.

Stephen's heart thumped with such intensity it felt like it was smashing against his ribcage. His hand juddered as he lifted the glass. The thought of what he was about to do terrified him. He was shaking so much that the glass tapped against his teeth as he poured the drink down his throat. Somehow, this stuff was even worse than the Scotch and tasted more like lighter fluid than antiseptic. The kick as it went down made him splutter and cough. He wiped his mouth on a jacket sleeve and put the glass back down. His hand had stopped shaking. The booze was beginning to have an effect.

The landlord chuckled. "I *did* warn you."

Laughter made his rubbery red face seem more friendly than it actually was, but his gaze remained cold and hostile. He glanced at the clock on the wall, which read ten minutes to last orders, and said: "Same again?"

"Yeah, why not?"

Then Stephen wondered if it might be better to speed up the process of getting pissed. "Actually, make it a triple."

The landlord smirked. "Somebody's really done a fuckin' number on you, fella?"

For a moment Stephen was terrified that the man knew his intentions, even though he knew that this wasn't possible. "Whatcha mean?"

The man rubbed a hand across his ham-coloured face and scratched at his veiny nose. "Well, I don't think you're celebrating, coz you've got a right fuckin' face on you," he said. "And judging by the way you're gagging whenever you down a drink, I don't think whisky's your thing. Which leaves drinking to dull the pain."

"Being married was pretty painful," Stephen said. He felt bad about lying.

A nasty smile stretched the landlord's thin lips. "But being divorced is worse, right?"

"Something like that."

2.

"WHERE'S THIS month's money?" Stella said.

Stephen sighed into the phone. "I'm working on it."

"You were working on it *last* month," she said. "Don't let this become a regular thing."

"I know I'm short. But I'm working on it. I didn't get as many hours as I thought I would."

"And I had to work longer hours to cover the kid's bills," Stella replied. "New shoes don't grow on trees, I'm sad to say. My Mum looked after them in the evenings, but you know how she is. She's in her seventies now, and her diabetes means she gets tired easily. I can't keep asking her to cover, and I can't afford a babysitter. And when I *do* get home, I'm too exhausted to spend much time with the kids. They're starting to feel like strangers. I can't keep doing this much longer."

"I know, I know. But Floyd promised me more hours this month. Plus some overtime."

"Speaking of promises, whatever happened to that promotion?"

"Don't, Stel. Just don't."

"I'm not the bad guy, Steve."

"I know you're not."

There wasn't a bad guy in their relationship. There were no arguments or affairs, and no dramatic moments that signalled the end. Instead, there was a gradual drift, like two unmoored boats pulling in separate directions, and their conversations grew more terse and monosyllabic. They worked increasingly long hours and spent fewer evenings together. They talked less about their futures and talked more about the kids. Soon they realised that the children were the only thing they had in common. Stephen moved out not long after and went to live in a flatshare with several other divorcees. They shared a tiny kitchen and a mouldy bathroom. It was depressing. Sometimes he heard his flatmates crying in the night. Sometimes he smothered his own tears with a pillow.

Even though the rent was cheap, London wasn't. Transport, food, bills, alimony, child support, and his share of the mortgage, all added up to more than he could afford. Stephen started juggling credit cards to help make ends meet – moving bills from one card to the other – and soon enough he was drowning in debt. He began skipping meals and public transport to bring his costs down. But whenever he seemed to be making a dent in his debts something happened that made things worse. One of the kids needed an urgent visit to the dentist, or they wanted to go on a school holiday, or the family car needed repairs, there was always a new problem that made Stephen's life a little more shitty.

"I'm just struggling at the moment," he said and reclined on his lumpy bed. "I've tried talking to Floyd but, let's be honest, he's a bit of a prick. And I've been looking at jobs, but there's not much out there for an unskilled forty-five-year-old. I promise I'll push him on the promotion."

Floyd hadn't promised him a promotion, he'd only hinted that it might be a possibility over time. Stephen exaggerated the story to give Stella some hope that his situation would get better. But now it was just another of his many regrets. He hadn't expected his ex-wife to cling to that sliver of hope with all her strength, to the point that it became the only thing she talked about. When he first told the lie, it didn't even cross Stephen's mind that what he was doing was cruel. But over time he realised what a dreadful mistake he'd made. But now it was too late to put the lie back in its box.

"What about the delivery job interview you had?"

"They didn't call me back."

"There must be some way of getting on top of your debts?"

"I could move back in."

Stella's drawn-out, uncomfortable silence told him everything he needed to know. "It'll be confusing for the kids. They might think we're getting back together. They've had enough upheaval recently, so they don't need any more, right now."

Stephen swallowed the hurt and disappointment. "Yeah, sure. I understand."

"I'm sorry."

"Don't worry about it," he said. "Besides, there might be a way to sort things out. But it's a bit of a long shot."

"What is it?"

An idea that had been bubbling away at the back of Stephen's mind since moving into the flatshare. It was the only thing he could think of to ensure his existence made any sense, to give his kids all the opportunities that he'd never had as a child.

"I'd rather not say, right now. But if it works, you and the kids will be sitting pretty for a very long time."

3.

STEPHEN KNOCKED back the triple in one grim swallow, but it fought him all the way down. As soon as it landed, the whiskey burned unpleasantly in his gut, like it was trying to eat through the lining and make its way back to the bottle.

This was the shot that finally had him wobbling on his feet. He gripped the bar for a moment as a lightheaded sensation washed over him. Now he was ready.

"Same again."

The landlord's eyes turned towards the clock. "This is the final one, fella. I'm calling last orders. That goes for everyone."

Stephen turned and looked around the lounge. He had to squint because the booze had made everything hazy and out of focus. The place was almost deserted, but at a small round table in the far corner of the room, three large men nursed their empty glasses and gazed back at him with predatory eyes. The biggest of them, with thick tattooed arms folded across his barrel chest, whispered something to his two friends and smirked. The two men laughed and performed 'same again' hand gestures towards the bar. The landlord let out a sad sigh and began pouring pints.

"You should leave," he whispered, as he placed the glasses on the countertop. "You don't need that final drink."

"Then just make it a double."

"I'm trying to do you a solid here."

"Then I'll drink it fast."

The landlord took the glass, poured a double, put it down in front of Stephen, and asked for the money.

As the big man with the tats approached the bar, Stephen delved in his trouser pockets and brought out a few coins and some pocket lint — far too little to pay for his drink. He smiled at the landlord.

"Actually, I don't think I've got enough cash."

The big man dropped a twenty on the bar, sneered in Stephen's direction, and picked up his pints. Stephen smiled back at the man and cocked a thumb in his direction.

"Looks like fat boy here's loaded. Put it on *his* tab."

The landlord's mouth dropped open. His eyes widened and he turned towards the big man. He started shaking his head. "Troy, leave it. The geezer's drunk. He doesn't know who he's fucking with."

4.

LES WALKED into the windowless little kitchen and nodded in Stephen's direction. "How's it going?"

"Can't complain," Stephen replied as he tucked into his microwave meal. "Well, I *could*, but nobody's gonna listen."

"Tell me about it," Les said. "And speaking of people who don't listen, have you seen Floyd on your travels?"

Stephen pointed up with his fork and jabbed it towards the ceiling. "He's up in his lair. Wasn't in the best of moods when I came in this morning."

"Probably hadn't had his daily wank."

Stephen laughed and choked on his curry.

Les' stern expression suggested he was being entirely serious.

"No joke, bruv. One of the cleaners caught him stroking one out in his office the other week."

"Really?"

"No shit. You know Nadia?"

Stephen had noticed her around the building. She was a plain, quiet, thirty-something woman who got on with her job with minimum fuss. They had exchanged brief smiles and the occasional hello. She didn't talk much.

"I've seen her around."

"She walked in on Floyd the other week. He'd left his door unlocked. He was cranking one out to some filth on Pornhub."

"That must have been embarrassing."

"You'd think," Les said with a shrug. "But Floyd just stood there with his dick in his hand, smiled, and asked her if she wanted to finish him off."

"Bullshit."

Les ran a hand across his shaved scalp and laughed. "It's fucking true."

"And did she?"

"Did she what?"

"You *know*? Finish him?

"Are you having a laugh, bruv? Course she fucking didn't. She took one look at Floyd's piece and told him she'd seen a bigger dick on her toddler. Then she walked out."

"Piss off. There's no way..."

"I'm serious. Talk to Irina. She and Nadia are proper tight. Nadia told Irina about it, and she told me."

Irina was another member of the cleaning crew. She had a sort-of-thing going with Les. They weren't quite in a relationship yet, but they had progressed beyond the friends-with-benefits stage. The pair stayed quiet about whatever it was that they were doing. Staff relationships were frowned upon.

"So what's Floyd gonna do about it?" Stephen asked.

"He's probably praying that Nadia keeps her mouth shut."

Les took something out of the fridge and threw it in the microwave. Whatever it was smelled awful, like blue cheese rotting inside a warm sewer pipe. It put Stephen off his last few bites of food. He put down the plate and looked at his colleague, who was smiling at something on his mobile phone screen.

"What's the hardest bar in London?"

Les looked up from his hand and frowned. "Whatcha wanna know a thing like that for?"

"Just curious," Stephen said with a shrug. "You seem to know these things?"

Les' expression hardened and his eyes went mean. "What? Coz I'm black?"

"Fuck no... Jesus... I was just... No, man..."

Les burst into laughter. "Your fucking face, man. I'm just fucking with ya."

Stephen remained silent for a few moments. He still wasn't quite able to process what had just happened. Realising that his little joke hadn't landed as anticipated, Les sat beside his colleague and said: "I was just messing about, bruv. I know you're not like some of the blokes in here. You asked about bars with reps, right?"

"Right."

"Why?"

"Coz one of my flatmates was talking about it the other day."

"Oh yeah? And what did *he* say?"

"Sez there's a gaff not far from Camberwell. An Irish bar. The kinda place where if your face doesn't fit they'll rearrange it for you."

"Especially if you're a brother."

"You've been there?"

"Nah, man. But a geezer I roll with has. He wandered in there to watch the footy. The fucking wasteman behind the bar took an instant dislike to him and told him to get the fuck out. Words were exchanged. Then fists were exchanged. Long story short, the poor bastard got fucking leathered by a couple of thick-necked Provo types."

"Sounds rough. So my flatmate's right?"

Les shook his head and patted Stephen on the shoulder. "Only if you're black, or maybe a member of the Orange Order."

"Oh, so you know somewhere better?"

Les pulled a face. "Better isn't a word I'd use for The Carpenter's Arms."

"Never heard of it."

"That's a good thing, bruv," Les said. "Up there, if your face don't fit, more likely than not they'd stab the fucking thing with a broken pint glass."

"Seriously?"

"Been two murders at The Carpenter's in the past five years. And shit's kicking off over there all the fuckin' time. The Po-po practically live on the doorstep."

"So how the hell is it still open?"

"By a fuckin' miracle. The landlord's on his last warning, apparently. All the glasses are plastic, even the shot glasses, coz the landlord doesn't wanna lose his licence. And they've even stopped serving bottles, or at least passing them to the customers to pour. A lad I know over in Finchley, Smithy, has been there a few times. Said there's a geezer in there, one of the regulars, Troy, who's proper fuckin' schitz, bruv. He's been in prison more times than he's had hot meals. The fucker's covered in prison tats."

"He sounds like fun."

Les snorted. "Maybe – if your idea of fun is getting your head stomped in. Seriously, the geezer's got an arrest sheet that's longer than my dick. Armed robbery, assault, burglary, and multiple cases of ABH and GBH. In fact, the bastard was even charged with murder once, but somehow managed to get off because there wasn't no witnesses, and they couldn't tie him to the scene with DNA."

"Jesus!"

Les shook his head. "Jesus wouldn't touch *that* place with a bargepole."

5.

TROY CAME in close and looked Stephen up and down like he was some sort of specimen. His cold blue eyes were expressionless, but he was breathing hard, and every time he exhaled his wide nostrils flared violently. The big man leaned forward until the tips of their noses were almost touching.

"You've got some fucking cheek on you, boy," he said.

Stephen swallowed his fears and sneered like he knew what he was doing. "I'm probably older than you, dickhead."

The landlord muttered *fuck me* under his breath, then slapped the countertop with his hand to get everyone's attention. "Seriously Troy, I can't be having this shit again. It'll cost me my fucking licence."

"I didn't start this shit."

"I know, but .."

"I'm gonna fucking finish it, though."

The landlord opened the till and put Troy's twenty back on the bar. "Listen up fellas, this round's on the house. Let's call it a night as friends."

"This loudmouthed sack of shit isn't my friend."

The landlord started pouring more pints to go with the ones Troy had put back on the countertop. "Let's put a fresh round in the mix," he said. "Leave the silly bastard alone, Troy. He isn't worth it."

The new drinks were enough to turn the big man's head. "You must really wanna keep that licence, Eric?"

"More than you'll ever know."

Troy fixed his hard gaze back on Stephen and jerked a thumb in the landlord's direction. "You should thank that geezer behind the bar. He just saved your life."

The big man moved towards his drinks as the landlord let out a long sigh of relief. Stephen began panicking as he realised that the whole situation was getting away from him. So he decided to go all in.

"Yeah, go on back to your girlfriends, you fat fuck."

The landlord let out a whimper. His red face was visibly draining of colour. "Oh, fuck me, now you've done it."

Troy looked almost regretful as he turned back to Stephen.

"Guess some people just don't like breathing."

6.

THE HANDSOME man in the slick pinstripe suit ran a hand through his expensively assembled haircut and said: "Well, obviously you're covered in the case of accidental death, murder, injuries that lead to you being unable to work (irreparable damage, basically), injuries caused to others, the usual stuff. However, you're not covered in cases of suicide or anything that involves an element of doubt."

"Doubt?"

The man tapped on his keyboard and looked at the monitor screen. "Well, for instance, let's say a suicide rigged to look like an accident."

Stephen smiled to disguise his unease. "Does that actually happen?"

"More than you might think."

"Really?"

"We call it Willy Loman Syndrome."

"Who?"

"Death of a Salesman?"

Stephen knew what the man was talking about but he shook his head and feigned ignorance.

"It's an Arthur Miller play. Pretty famous. Willy Loman takes out an insurance policy with the intention of killing himself so his family can inherit."

"Oh."

"Not a fan of the theatre?"

Stephen shrugged. "Not on my salary."

"Basically, somebody takes an insurance policy and crashes their car, or plunges headfirst off their house roof when there's no good reason for them to be up there, or has the kind of *accident* that lines 'em up for a Darwin Award. If there's an element of doubt we don't pay, or at the very least we fight like hell to make sure we can avoid it. The same goes for disappearances. If somebody disappears, then there's an element of doubt, and we don't pay."

"Well, I kinda like living," Stephen said with a smile. "But coz I work as a security guard I figure I'd better sort myself out, you know?"

"Totally understand, Mr Cresswell. It pays to be covered."

"Last month, a fella in our company was stabbed by a kid trying to nab some laptops. He wasn't covered and his family got nothing more than his final month's pay."

The man nodded. "You do realise that because of the nature of your job, you'll have to pay a larger premium."

"Of course."

"Can you afford it?"

Stephen blanched slightly when he saw the monthly payments, but smiled and nodded. "Not a problem. Piece of cake."

7.

TROY MOVED back towards Stephen and stood within striking distance. His icy blues were hard and unblinking. Stephen tried to maintain eye contact but there was a fierceness in the other man's gaze that was almost too much to bear. Eventually, Stephen had to turn away. He looked down into his drink and wondered if there was a better solution to his problems than this.

"D'you wanna repeat what you just said, dickhead?"

"You mean about you being a fat fuck?"

Troy threw back his head and laughed. "You've got some fucking nads on you, fella. I'll give you that much."

Eric slammed his hand against the countertop again. "I said leave it, Troy. This moron's off his tits. It's not worth it."

Troy eyeballed the landlord. "Next time you tell me to leave it, I'll be leaving you on the floor in a pool of your own fucking blood."

Eric edged back from the bar and decided it was healthier not to get involved in what was going to happen. He held up his hands to illustrate his neutrality.

"You're on your own, geez."

Then the landlord turned his back and went through a door next to the drinks display, saying: "I'm not watching my licence go down the shitter."

Troy glanced at his friends and gave them the nod. Stephen heard a door bolt slam into place. The big man shuffled his shoulders a few times and grinned.

It was on.

Stephen dropped his right shoulder to launch a right hook, but Troy was faster. The big man hit him in the stomach with a couple of rapid jabs that had Stephen staggering back. He held his gut, which hurt like hell, and tried to act nonchalant about it.

"Is that all you've got, fat boy?"

Troy winked at his friends. "I'll say something for this prick, he's definitely got some big fuckin' bollocks on him."

Stephen's vision blurred and the world seemed to wobble. Something warm and wet flowed over his hand. It only took a quick glance to confirm how much trouble he was in. Blood streamed through his fingers and splashed the floorboards. Stephen knew he'd been stabbed, but something about it was too surreal for his mind to accept. He raised his hand in the air and turned it, still not believing the evidence of his eyes, but there was nothing fake about the blood-slicked surface of his palm.

Then he noticed the small-bladed knife in Troy's hand.

The big man smiled at his handiwork, then he went behind the bar and knocked on Eric's door. "Come on out, mate."

"And do what?" bellowed the landlord. "Watch you wipe your arse with my fucking licence?"

"You're not gonna lose a thing, dickhead. Get out here now before I come in there and beat seven shades of shit outta you."

Eric emerged from behind the door slowly and observed the mess on the other side of the bar. Then he closed his eyes briefly, shook his head, and let out a sigh. "You didn't need to do this."

Stephen wasn't sure who the landlord was talking to. Maybe it was directed at both of them.

Troy clicked his fingers in front of the landlord's face. "Open the cellar."

Eric turned around and rushed through the door. Stephen heard the sound of something slamming at the back of the pub, probably the cellar door.

Troy winked at Stephen, then rushed in and hit him with another flurry of knife work. All his fight was gone, so he didn't bother with defending himself. He acted like a dispassionate observer of his own demise. Stephen's nonchalance made his assailant angrier and forced him to work harder. Eventually, Troy pulled away and watched his victim sway like a sapling in a strong breeze. His eyes blazed with hatred and confusion like he expected fear or tears or anything that would validate what had just happened. Instead, Stephen grinned at him and spat blood on the floor.

"Why the fuck won't he go down, Gal?"

"Dunno, mate."

"You dunno much, do you?"

Troy turned his attention to his friend who shuffled nervously and shrugged in confusion. The big man shook his head in disgust. "What's the fucking point of you?"

Stephen knew that he should have been on his back by now, getting a last view of the nicotine-stained plasterwork. The only thing keeping him on his feet was the knowledge that his kids would be well looked after by the insurance. When he realised that it was over, and he didn't need to stay upright anymore, Stephen stumbled and sat down on the floorboards with a thump. He collapsed on his back and blinked at the ceiling. The taste of blood was in his mouth and its scent filled his nostrils. He knew the end was close.

Troy clicked his fingers at his friends and grabbed one of Stephen's legs.

"Help me pick this piece of shit up."

The three bruisers grabbed the prone man, heaved him up by his limbs and carried him through the pub. Stephen's head was bashed several times as they rounded corners and went through doors. He wanted to cry out in pain, but he refused to give them the satisfaction. They dropped him on the floor outside the cellar door.

"I don't need this," Eric said. "Just take him somewhere and dump him."

"Gimme a couple of hours, and no fucker'll ever know he was here."

Stephen realised what they had planned and began to panic. He tried to scream for help, but he didn't have the strength to raise his voice by much more than a whisper. Even so, Troy silenced him by dropping to his knees and slamming the knife into his stomach again. The blow silenced him. Stephen tried to catch his breath but choked and coughed, tasting yet more blood. A chill spread across his body, leaving him to wonder if it was the beginning of the end.

Troy grabbed his feet and somebody seized his wrists. They hoisted Stephen off the ground, swung once and let him go. A brief, pleasant moment of weightlessness was replaced by the pull of gravity as he fell through the darkness. Stephen braced for impact but the shock of the landing still brought fresh suffering. One of his arms broke with a loud crack as he hit the steps and started rolling. A white-hot burst of agony shot through his chest, and then there was another lightning flash of pain as his right leg shattered. When Stephen finally hit the floor, the air left his lungs in one long rush. His survival instinct kicked in and he tried gasping for breath but the strength wasn't there. He considered putting his hands down, so he could push himself up off the floor, but he couldn't move at all. He was paralysed.

Upstairs, Troy's voice carried: "Get something sharp... Find some meat knives from the kitchen... It's your fucking pub, Eric. How the fuck would I know?"

At that moment, Stephen knew he was going to disappear. There would be no insurance money for his children. All he would leave them with were large debts and a few memories that would fade with time. He wondered if they would see him as a coward who ran away from his responsibilities. Stephen reflected on his wasted life and began crying.

None of this was fair. Who would look after his kids now?

A darkness that was colder and blacker than any pub cellar enveloped him, and white noise buzzed angrily in his ears. Spots danced in front of his eyes before they darkened and spread and obscured the last of his vision.

The last thing Stephen heard, almost inaudible through the ever-increasing buzz, was the sound of feet as they stomped down the stairs.

MARTIN STANLEY

SIX SHOOTER

A MAN CALLED MARY

(A STANTON BROTHERS' STORY)

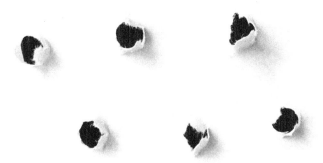

Originally intended as a sort of companion piece to *Fighting Talk* (regular readers will see what I mean), setting up the Stanton brothers for the events of *Bad Luck and Trouble*, *A Man Called Mary* is the one tale in this collection in which I had no idea where it was going. I fell in love with Mary's first paragraph (originally planned as the opening salvo of the story) and tried to take it from there, but it wasn't having any of it. Unable to get it further forward than the first few thousand words, I put it back down for a few years while working on other manuscripts.

The story refused to progress any further without Eric Stanton's input. Then Billy Chin elbowed his way to the table without being invited and decided that the story wasn't going forward unless he had his say. My original ending, a somewhat happier one, grew fainter with every ill-judged decision Mary and Raffles made.

This is probably the first thing I've written that has been done completely on-the-fly. None of my original ideas and plot points made it to the end of the first draft. Something I realised, when I looked at the manuscript before starting on the second draft, was that I started writing it properly in June 2023 when I found out that my dog, Olive, had advanced kidney disease. I think some of that darkness filtered through the bedrock of my subconscious and into the storyline.

There are some laughs here, and Eric's and Derek's banter and quips still pack a punch, but this is a darker affair than I originally intended. That's not to say I feel like this is a lesser affair. It isn't. In fact, I bloody love this tale. It's one of my favourite stories featuring the brothers. I wouldn't have put it at the end of the collection if I thought it was a piece of shit. Always end with your strongest story, so they say, and leave 'em wanting more.

An eye for an eye makes the whole world blind
Mohandas Karamchand Gandhi
(at least, attributed to him)

PART ONE: FATE

1.

IT'S FUNNY how life works, isn't it?

Our fates often hang on split-second decisions. Taken without thought, or experience, the wrong ones can be fatal. Choosing to shout during an argument when it might be smarter to stay calm can be the difference between walking away unharmed or going in the ground. Saying I love you love at the wrong time can kill a relationship just as surely as infidelity. Going left when all signs are pointing right can be the difference between the opportunity of a lifetime or outright disaster, meeting the love of your life or going home alone, and sometimes it's as simple as life or death.

Take us, for example. If we'd arrived at his home even a minute later, our boss would've been dead. Alan Piper's life would be over if my brother hadn't taken it upon himself to break Henry Mansell's arm over a ten grand debt, instead of trying to do things my way and talk him into coughing up the cash. Although, if Piper had died that night, this might've been the best result for everyone. There would definitely be a lower body count.

But that's not how shit happens in the real world. In fact…

It's funny how life works, isn't it?

2.

HENRY MANSELL waved his hands around to get his point across. Every gesticulation sent his shaggy hair in several different directions at once. His baggy Henley shirt, garishly patterned in yellow and green Paisley, flapped as he stomped around the candlelit room. Whenever he swung his arms to make a point, the candles flickered and hissed and heightened the already overpowering scent of vanilla.

"Whyn'tcha lissen to *my* side of the story?"

"I don't give a fuck about *your* side, Hen. It'll just be more bullshit. Last time I checked, stupid fuckin' excuses weren't legal tender, so you might wanna magic up some money, and fast."

"There's two sides to every story, gadge."

"You're right. There *are* two sides to every story. But you remain a cunt in both of them."

That made my brother chuckle. It didn't take much to make him laugh. Sometimes it was as simple as dropping the c-bomb at the right point in a conversation.

Henry had borrowed fifteen grand from our boss in order to fulfil his dream of becoming a porn director. But like most ill-considered dreams it met cold, hard reality, along with a complete lack of talent and common sense, and nosedived into the ground.

Henry spent a couple of grand on fancy video rigs he couldn't use, then he dropped the same again on a bunch of guys with big dicks and small brains, and spaffed another grand on somebody who *could* use the cameras. Realising she was going to be the unpaid centrepiece in an unscripted bareback six-man gangbang, Henry's girlfriend wisely decided to grab the cash and do a runner. It was a smart move on her part.

The dealer took the collapse of both the dream and his relationship pretty hard and made a more foolish choice. Because the girl had taken the dosh, Henry decided that it was no longer his problem to deal with. If our boss wanted his money he'd have to get it from the ex-partner, despite the fact that Henry sold enough pills, weed, and gak to cover the amount in a couple of weeks.

The boss had been fair for a while. His friendship with Henry was strong enough for him to overlook a couple of missed payments, but it didn't last a third. That was when he sent us. No more excuses. No more broken promises. We either came back with some money, or we left him somewhere with broken bones.

I'd had enough of cracking limbs, so I decided to see what diplomacy got me.

And what it got me was this fucking idiot, waving his arms around like we were the problem.

"Whyn'tcha out chasing Marie?"

"Coz she didn't borrow the money."

"She fuckin' swiped it though."

"That's *your* problem, Hen. They call it caveat emptor."

"Cavvy what?"

"It means don't borrow off Alan Piper if you're not gonna pay him back."

"Like I sez, Marie's gorrit. Sort it out with…."

I got in close. "Listen, dickhead, we're not here for an argument, we're here to get paid. Otherwise, I'm gonna let the big lad in to give you our counter-argument. And I think you know how that's gonna go."

My brother shuffled his shoulders, made his enormous hands into fists and went up on tiptoes to accentuate his nearly six-five frame. He was ready to start breaking things.

Henry now understood the problem. His friendship with Piper was over. The old rules no longer applied. He was now just another sucker. And Alan Piper had no time for suckers.

The man swiped his hands through the air, generating a fresh breeze that made the candles flutter again. "Fuckin' fine. I'm gonna gerris money, lads. Butcha gorra gimme more time."

"No more time," I said. "No more excuses. You either gimme at least five hundred, or summat's getting broken. And I don't mean your fuckin' heart."

He kept gesturing and stomping. "You know who you're messing with here? My boss has Piper on fuckin' speed dial. Just one call and I'll have youse buried. I'll… ."

My brother shuffled forward and threw a right hook that put out Henry's lights along with most of the fancy candles. Then he dragged him upright and slapped him awake. "Listen up, you Grizzly Adams-looking piece of shite, you either get that fuckin' money or I'm gonna snap your scrawny arm like a twig."

There was fear on Henry's face. This was a new sensation for him. In his line of business he was usually the prick with the power, the one laying down the law, so he understood how precarious his position was. The man tried a fawning grimace of a smile and softened his tone. "Lads, I can gerrit for youse in a couple of days. Butcha gorra trust us, like."

It was the sucker's refrain. Everything was always in a couple of hours, days, weeks, but never when you needed it. And they always insisted that you trust them.

We decided not to.

Instead, my brother threw Henry back on the ground, gripped his right forearm and hammered it with a heavy cosh until it broke. As the man rolled around the shagpile and screamed in agony, my brother shrugged his huge shoulders and said: "You might wanna tell us where that money is, sweetheart. We're not leaving until you do. But I wanna be somewhere tonight, and you're getting in the way of that, so I'm gonna work fast. If you don't talk, I'm gonna snap all your limbs, then I'm gonna shave off your stupid fuckin' hair, coz it's pissing me right off."

It was the hair that settled it.

Henry shrieked out the hiding place.

Pleased with himself, my brother smirked in my direction. "We did it your way for long enough. Now let's get Piper's shit and get going."

I went into the bedroom, walked past an ornate four-poster bed, and over to a refurbished Victorian radiator. I knelt beside it and prised up a loose floorboard with a penknife blade. I reached inside, pushed my fingers through a carpet of spiderwebs and dust bunnies, and found what I was searching for.

It was a small, decorative tea caddy. I removed the lid and pulled out a couple of thick wads of notes wrapped tightly with elastic. A quick count put it in the region of twenty grand. I took what Henry owed and threw the rest on the bed. My brother eyed the cash on the duvet and chewed his bottom lip nervously.

"We could take that," he said. "Split it between us."

"If we start raiding Piper's customers, we won't live very long."

My brother snorted. "You're misunderestimating us."

"I don't give a fuck how tough you think you are, Derek, nobody's harder than a bullet. And that's exactly what Piper'll use on us if we start putting the squeeze on his regulars."

My brother grumbled something abusive under his breath as we went back into the living room. Henry wasn't moving. I checked his pulse, which was fine, and put a pillow under his head. We'd already broken his arm and got what we came for, so there was no need for further damage.

My brother huffed. "Whyn't you just wank him off, while you're at it?"

"Why don't you go fuck yourself, instead?"

"Yeah, well, if we don't get a shift on, that's *exactly* what I'm gonna be doing."

3.

WE RACED towards Piper's place near Yarm. My brother went into the turns too fast, and fishtailed through traffic with scant regard for safety. His foot spent too much time on the accelerator and not enough on the brakes. I'd been white-knuckling the door handle for the last fifteen minutes and my heart rate was into the hundreds.

"What's the hurry?"

"Janine fuckin' Sterling, that's who."

"Is she worth dying for?" I said. "Coz I don't wanna end up in a bodybag on account of your latest one night stand."

"Fuck that shit. My car, *my* rules. You want out, open the door and jump. Besides, she's not just a one night stand, she's *the* one night stand."

"Who's her pimp?"

"Fuck you, gadge. You know I don't pay for action. Women should be paying *me*, you know what I mean? Besides, she's not a prozzie, even if she fucks like one. Swear down, she looks like a model."

"If she has all her teeth she'll be an improvement on the last one."

My brother tutted and gave me an angry glance. "They were *grills*. That shit goes *over* the teeth."

"From the looks of 'em, they wanna be going in the fuckin' bin."

"The fuck? It's a fashion statement. You wouldn't understand, granddad, but that shit's trendy now."

"I'm fuckin' three years older than you," I said. "Besides, if you wanna bang someone with metal teeth, that's your business. Why the hell do I care? I just didn't realise that looking like summat outta fuckin' Moonraker was all the rage nowadays. Is everyone getting metal teeth now?"

"You know summat, I was thinking of getting some?"

"Yeah? Just don't expect me to go down the town with you when you're wearing 'em."

"Wozzat supposed to mean?"

"How many places are you banned from now?"

"Wozzat gotta do with owt?"

"You're not the most even-tempered person," I said. "Last time you got banned, it was coz you beat the fuck outta some bouncer for putting his hand on your tit and telling you to calm down when you were trying to push in the queue. God knows what'd happen if one of those idiots started taking the piss outta your smile."

Derek shook his head and said: "You know summat, we wouldn't even be here talking about this shit if Gordy had got his fat arse in gear and heeded his master's call."

My brother was right. When Piper wanted damage to be done, we'd always be second choice to Gordy Willis. Piper's pet thug loved his work. It gave him a reason to get up in the morning. Every punch he landed put a bigger smile on his face, and every broken bone put an extra spring in his step. Gordy didn't care who he walloped. Pensioners, pregnant women, the chronically sick, the terminally ill, they were all equally worthless in Gordy's opinion and all as deserving of the rough stuff. Henry Mansell was lucky that Gordy wasn't answering his phone, and that he got us instead, because Piper's pet would have relished turning his bones to powder.

My brother slowed as we approached Piper's place. Then he eased to a crawl when we reached the open front gate.

"That's odd," he said.

It wasn't odd, it was trouble. I reached into my jeans pocket and removed a cosh, then I pulled a switchblade from my brother's glovebox and pressed the button. His eyes fixed on the knife, and he sighed sadly. "Guess I'm not gonna be seeing Janine tonight, am I?"

"Unlikely," I replied.

"Fucksake."

Alan never opened his gate to unwanted visitors. Sometimes, he didn't even extend the courtesy to his invited guests, which meant somebody had used either technical wizardry or bought the entry code to gain access. There was something a bit more old-fashioned keeping the gates open. Wooden wedges, jammed in tight, gave them an easy escape route. This was planned.

I got out of the car and sprinted down a gravel path into the estate with my brother hot on my heels. The narrow road soon widened into a vast driveway that rolled right up to the front steps of our boss' mansion. Beside this was a half-acre, tree-lined lawn that was being drowned by an industrial sized sprinkler. Three men raced around beneath the spray, slipping and sliding comically, as they each tried to catch the person in front of them. It was like a Benny Hill sketch but with more blood and fewer tits. One of the men was Piper, grimacing in pain, wearing a sliced up, bloodied T-shirt and pyjama bottoms that were soaked with water and claret, along with two idiots dressed all in black, with balaclavas over their heads. Whenever they got close, the intruders slashed out at Piper with meat knives. One of the intruders slipped and landed face first on the grass, his partner tripped over a trailing leg and went sliding across the turf like it was a party flume. This gave Piper the chance to make a break for it. Because of the pain, his progress was sluggish as he shuffled towards the exit. When Alan saw us, he let out a scream of joy, and yelled for help.

My brother brushed past the boss and charged towards the lawn. The moment his feet hit the turf, my brother lost his balance and slid across the surface until he came to a stop near one of the intruders, who took the opportunity to swing out wildly and slice him across the shoulder. The big lad roared angrily and landed a right hook that had his attacker staggering like a piss head at Happy Hour. Then he grabbed Balaclava's knife hand and squeezed it until he let go of the blade. Despite disarming his assailant, my brother maintained his grip and crushed the man's fingers like they were pretzel sticks. By the time Balaclava started squealing for help, his fingers were bent in ways that nature hadn't intended.

The other intruder held his leg as he struggled to his feet, then he wobbled unsteadily towards the two struggling men and jabbed his blade into my brother's side. Derek yelped, turned, and pushed his attacker away. Then he fell on his back and scrambled out of trouble. The man pulled his injured associate off the ground and dragged him towards the exit. I started to give chase, but Alan grabbed my forearm and held on tightly. "I need a doctor," he said. "They can wait. Gemme inside."

My brother staggered to his feet and lifted his t-shirt. There was a gash in his right oblique that oozed blood. Then he looked at his injured shoulder, and squeezed the area around the wound. Neither injury would require anything more than a few stitches, some dressings, and antibiotics. When he'd finished inspecting himself, he approached Piper, lifted him like he was a newborn baby and carried him towards the house.

"Who were they?" he said.

"How the fuck would I know," Piper barked. "I wasn't wearing me X-ray specs, was I?"

Even at his most vulnerable, the loan shark remained an insufferable prick. Derek growled and said: "Talk to me like that again and I'll drop you on your fuckin' head."

Alan tightened his grip around the big lad's neck and mumbled a hasty apology.

My brother kicked the front door open and walked through a grand, double-height entrance hall. We veered right into a hangar-sized living room and he lowered the injured man towards the sofa. Alan yelped in what we thought was pain, but then said: "That's Italian leather, gadge."

My brother hissed under his breath and moved in the direction of another sofa on the opposite side of the room that looked a little more beaten up and lived in. Alan shook his head again: "Not there. That's an original Remy Marceau."

"For fucksake, is there anywhere I *can* put you in this fuckin' museum?" my brother yelled. "Coz if you don't say where you wanna go soon, you're going in the fuckin' bin."

"That chaise longue over there," he said. "It's the wife's favourite."

My brother dropped Piper onto a blue velvet lounger that he immediately smeared with blood.

"Shame to ruin a nice chair," I said.

Alan winced. "She's out right now, chowing down on some guy's tubesteak. She could do with a little suffering."

I lifted his t-shirt and surveyed the damage. They were mostly flesh wounds. A long jagged slash just above the waistband of his pyjamas oozed blood, but it wasn't deep enough to affect any major veins or arteries. One nasty gash allowed us to take a peek at a couple of Alan's ribs, but the damage didn't go any further than this. There was a gaping incision in his right pec, where someone had tried, and failed, to put a blade through his heart. Another laceration in the left shoulder went down into the muscle and seemed to have nicked a vein. If it had been an artery, Piper would already be dead.

"Get Frenchy on the phone," he said, his eyes closing. "He'll fix me up."

As I went to move away and make the call, Alan came awake again and grasped my forearm in a steel grip. "And find Gordy Willis," he said. "That fat fuck was the only other person with the entry code."

Then he passed out.

PART TWO: MARY

1.

NOBODY CALLS their son Mary, certainly not in this town, if they want him to have the best start in life. And so it was with the man called Mary, sitting hunched over a half-finished pint at one of the back tables in the Sun and Moon. His parents had christened him with the far more sensible moniker of Shawn Wilcox. It was a name that stuck with him for thirty years, until the day he crossed paths with a vicious crew called Hilda's Boys.

They'd taken exception to his habit of using their patch of wasteland on the old St Hilda's estate as a shortcut to get home from work. The way The Boys saw it, they'd spent months battling to secure this territory from local rivals and they sure as hell weren't going to let some random working man cut through their domain unless he paid for the privilege.

The first time they caught Shawn on their turf, they warned him politely. They chased him down Lower East Street, wrestled him to the ground, and screamed in his face they wouldn't be so nice the next time around. The second time, they stopped being polite, dropped him on the deck with some gut shots, blackened both his eyes, and threw him in a pile of dog shit. The third and final time, The Boys dragged Shawn onto a patch of wild grass in the shade of the old Town Hall and beat him with baseball bats, brick-halves, steel toe caps and fists. They turned him from a pretty boy into a pretty ugly one and put him in a coma for several weeks. The surgeon tasked with putting his face back together seemed to have studied his trade at the Picasso school of anatomy, because he performed the kind of reconstruction job that would have made the Cubist painter proud. Of course, Shawn didn't know this until the first time he looked in the mirror. Just one glance was enough for him to wish they'd put him back to sleep permanently.

His wife left him and took their baby girl — saying it wasn't right for the child to see what had happened to its father. Then he lost his restaurant job, because customers complained that his presence was putting them off their food. His hideously disfigured face prevented employers from giving him a job. The lack of income meant his money ran dry and he missed so many mortgage payments that the bank had no choice but to send in the bailiffs to take his home. The only bit of good luck saving him from the street was a belated insurance payout that disappeared far too soon on food and rent.

It took a while for Shawn to summon the courage to show his face in the local bars again. His presence alone was enough to empty most establishments. It was the kind of mug you imagined in horror novels.

And one book in particular…

The resemblance was noted by an especially well-read pisshead with a tar-black sense of humour. He approached Shawn's table, leaned in close, smirked knowingly, then raised his arms aloft and yelled joyfully: "It's alive."

Then he turned to the rest of the bar and announced: "I'm Victor Frankenstein, and it's with great pride that I present to you tonight's special guest: Mary Shelley's Shawn Wilcox."

It got big laughs, and the name caught on.

Soon enough it was whittled down to just Mary Shelley, then, after a few weeks, it became the even snappier title of Mary.

And the moniker stuck.

It was just another drop of bad luck in a life that had long since drowned in the stuff.

Mary tore a damp beer mat to pieces without even realising he was doing it and pondered his latest misfortune: a ten grand debt to a particularly unpleasant loan shark. He was several weeks behind on his payments and looking at a serious beating, possibly even a broken bone or two, because Alan Piper didn't like having to chase debtors. He particularly hated having to harass addicts of any kind. In his opinion, if you have the money to fund a habit, you can afford to pay your debts on time.

Mary was a gambler. And although he didn't believe he was an addict, he certainly craved the excitement and adrenaline of a good Poker game. Most of his wins felt anticlimactic; the real pleasure was in the moments leading up to victory — or the vinegar strokes, as he liked to call them. The way he saw it, he deserved to get some pleasure out of his occupation. After everything he'd been through, he was entitled to some excitement, even if it was just a means to an end.

Mary's ultimate goal was the money he needed to fix his face. He started devouring books on Poker (especially Texas Hold'em) and the strategies needed to win. During long sleepless nights, when his face ached, and he felt particularly bitter about his life, he memorised cards and devised game plans. He got good enough to win regularly in small games against suckers and novices. Over time, the opponents got better and the stakes got bigger, and as the months passed he built up a ten grand stash.

It would have been easy to maintain the slow and steady path of amassing smaller amounts over several years, travelling the country for lower stakes games, but Mary didn't have the patience. He wanted the hundred grand he believed would restore his face to something approaching its former glory as soon as he could earn it. The only way to do this was by playing for bigger stakes against better opponents.

Mary took his stash to a regular closed door poker session held in the back room of a bar owned by Piper. It cost a grand just to get through the door. Games started with a five hundred stake and went up from there. The room was hot and sweaty and dark. Red faced men concentrated on the cards in front of them and occasionally pushed chips into the centre of the tables they were hunched over. Mary got over his initial sugar rush of excitement and cashed in on a table of tired-looking, sad-faced blokes. Nobody commented on his appearance. It made him want to cry with happiness. After the warm glow subsided, Mary got on with the cold business of relieving them of their money.

At one point in the evening Mary could have cashed out with fifty grand, but he kept pushing his luck until it couldn't be pushed anymore. The losses started gradually but they accumulated quickly until his fifty grand was worth only half that.

This was when the voice of reason begged him to walk away, telling him that twenty five grand was a fifteen grand profit. But like all addicts on the slippery slope, he ignored this voice in favour of the other one; the one that flips good news on its head. *You've lost twenty-five grand. Don't accept that shit and walk away. You're good enough to get back to fifty*, it said.

It took just over an hour for him to regret this decision. His attempt to bluff a better player, cost him not only his original twenty-five but another ten grand on top of that — money he didn't have. He begged Alan Piper for a loan, which he promised to repay at the standard rate.

He thanked his benefactor, who warned him without smiling, that he'd expect the first payment in a week.

That was five weeks ago.

Mary continued playing smaller games, but his touch had temporarily deserted him. Decisions that once seemed easy became wars of attrition. He still managed to win more than he lost, but his profits were swallowed up by Piper's debt, and the financial hole he was in deepened. He missed his first payment, but promised a double payment for the next week.

Piper told him he'd better have it.

He didn't have it.

Nor did he have the one after that, which prompted Piper to take action.

This came in the form of Derek Stanton, who threw a one-two combination to the face that had him spitting teeth, followed by another blow to the kidneys that dropped Mary on the deck and ensured he pissed blood for the next few days.

As he was leaving, Derek told Mary he'd been told to pull his punches, before warning him about the kind of damage another missed payment would bring.

This gave Mary all the incentive he needed to run until he had the money. His face was too distinctive for him to move around, but it wouldn't stop him from hiding for a few weeks while he rebuilt his savings. He crashed with a friend in a small flat a stone's throw from Linthorpe Road. The place was a mouldy shithole with bad plumbing, and his friend wasn't happy about being a babysitter. Jezza demanded that Mary pay for his smokes, smack, and snacks, but he was kind enough to venture out and buy their supplies, even though he complained and grumbled about it.

Gradually, Jezza grew tired of this arrangement and threw him out. Mary visited another friend, Raffles (so named because he once lifted the proceeds of a church raffle to fund his heroin habit), who was more amenable to his predicament.

In exchange for the money he needed to buy his fixes, Raffles made sure Mary had a bed to sleep in and food in the fridge. Mary kept his side of the bargain by playing online poker against a succession of losers. As long as he kept the stakes small, there seemed to be a never-ending stream of suckers without the experience to play strategically or the sense to know when they were dealing with a better player. The winnings weren't high, but they were enough to cover Raffles' addiction, their food bills, and some money towards the debt.

But hiding in a dirty bedsit with barely enough floor space between the bed and the kitchenette became boring very quickly. Despite Raffles' warnings about taking unnecessary risks, Mary ventured outside for ever longer periods, visiting local pubs for a pint, or cafes for mugs of coffee and plates of greasy food.

Mary knew the dangers: Alan obviously had people out looking for him, and there were always scumbags willing to snitch him out in exchange for cash or favours. Despite the pull of his addiction, and the desire to fleece ever more suckers, Mary couldn't spend every waking moment in that horrible room. He needed a change of scenery.

So it wasn't all that surprising when the Stanton brothers came through the entrance of the Sun and Moon and stared right at him. Both men were well built, with physiques that showed the benefits of long hours at the gym, and looked similar, with olive skin, dark stubble and large brown eyes. Eric stood about average height; Derek towered over him at six-four and a half, plus he was almost twice as wide — his shoulders looked like two boulders beneath his black leather jacket.

A paralysing mixture of fear and acceptance kept Mary in his seat. His eyes went to the second exit. If he really wanted it, he knew he could beat the brothers to the door, but the odds were good that they already knew where he was crashing.

Eric sat beside Mary. Derek dragged a chair from another table and rested his bulk on it. The legs creaked beneath his weight. They kept their mouths shut and watched him drink. Mary tried ignoring them until the silence became too toxic for him to ignore.

"Tell Alan I'll have his money soon."

Eric shook his head. "Too late for that."

"I just need a week."

"You needed a week a month ago."

"I can get his money."

"You shouldn't have run."

Mary's gaze fixed on the big man, then he shivered. "I didn't want him to hit me again."

Derek chuckled until his brother fixed him with a cold stare. When he had everyone's attention, Eric replied:

"He's the least of your worries. Alan *can* be reasonable if you stand your ground, but runners really piss him off."

"But…"

"You ran, Mary. Alan won't forgive that shit."

"I just needed more time."

"We all need more time."

"Be reasonable, mate."

"I *am* being reasonable. Derek wants to fuck you up. I'm the only thing preventing that from happening."

"So Alan can do it later."

Eric shrugged and looked towards the bar. The barman ushered out a few afternoon drinkers and bolted the door shut. He put a sign in the window that read *Closed: staff training day* and began drawing the curtains.

"You shouldn't have borrowed if you couldn't pay," Eric said. "And you certainly shouldn't have vanished."

"Have a heart, man."

Eric let his hands fall on the table. "If it was up to me, I'd let you walk. But it isn't."

"Is Alan coming here?"

Eric nodded.

"*I'm* staff training?"

"Summat like that."

Mary's hands trembled as he lifted the last of the beer to his lips. The edge of the glass tapped against his broken teeth, sending bolts of pain deep into his gums. Then the bottom of the glass went *tap-tap-tap* against the tabletop as Mary lowered his hand.

Eric clicked his fingers at the barman, who looked up from the table he was cleaning with a dirty rag.

"Get me a pint and a whisky chaser."

The man shook his head. "I'm not serving."

Eric scowled. "I don't remember *asking* for those drinks, fella. It was a demand not a request."

"Alan said nothing for *him*."

"They're not for him, they're for me."

The man slow-walked to the bar and poured the drinks. He brought the glasses over to where they were sitting, slammed them down, and stormed away. He glared at Eric as he resumed wiping puddles of beer off a nearby tabletop.

Eric pushed the booze towards Mary.

The barman stood upright, squeezing the rag in his fists. Droplets of beer spotted the floorboards.

Realising that violence was about to occur, Derek got to his feet and took a couple of steps in the barman's direction. The change of opponent made the barman flinch and retreat to the safety of the bar. He wiped the counter top and eyed the big man warily.

Derek pointed at him. "Say another fuckin' word, baldilocks, and I'll break your shiny fuckin' head open."

The barman focused on the counter until the big man turned away and sat down again.

Mary downed the shot in one, felt the burn at the back of his throat, gagged and coughed. "Where's Alan?"

"About five minutes away."

Mary's bottom lip trembled and tears collected in his long eyelashes, which he wiped with a shaky hand. "I didn't mean to run. I got scared."

Eric gave the man's shoulder a gentle pat. "I believe you, but you should save it for Alan."

"Will he listen?"

Eric lifted his arms and let them fall, suggesting it might go either way.

"I'm fucked, aren't I?"

"Probably."

Just as Mary began speaking, the door opened and Alan Piper walked in. He wore a slick grey suit of handcrafted Italian silk, a world-class haircut, and designer black brogues. He was almost too pretty to be a villain, with his sharp cheekbones, angular jaw, and big green eyes, he looked more like a fashion model. He even had a catwalk strut. The smile he flashed when he saw Mary slouched beside Eric was as flawless as the rest of him.

A tall, fat man with lank black hair that matched his baggy shellsuit fell in beside Alan and glared at the brothers.

"Why'd you buy this shitbag drinks?" he said, pointing at Mary.

Eric grinned. "Because of free will, Gordy. Summat you wouldn't understand."

Gordy Willis scowled. "The boss dun't pay you for free will."

"I exercised it anyway."

"Well, in't that clever of you?"

"You've got a funny idea about what's clever, Gord," Eric said. "The man needed a drink and I bought him one."

"The boss said no drinks."

Eric sighed. "One drink isn't gonna hurt."

Alan nodded. "But disobeying orders could."

The threat of violence got Derek off his seat again. He sidled in towards his brother and made sure that Alan and Gordy got a good view of his fists. The pair caught the vibes coming off the big lad and decided not to push the issue further. Neither man was suicidal.

"Ah, fuck it. Give him everything behind the bar, if you wanna," Alan said. "After all it's a celebration, innit?"

"What're we celebrating?" Derek asked.

"Alan's just fucked another one of his waitresses," Eric replied. "Break out the Champers."

Derek threw back his head and roared with laughter. Alan tried smiling but it was humourless. "You two clowns are joking your way to the dole queue."

"That'll be summat to cheer," Gordy added.

"Won't it just? Now where the fuck was I?"

"A celebration," Eric said.

Alan flashed his perfect smile — this time the humour had returned. "Oh, that's right. We've finally caught Arnie," he replied, wafting his hand towards Mary.

Mary wore a bemused expression. "Arnie?"

"As in Schwarzenegger?" Derek asked.

"That's right," Alan responded irritably. "What of it?"

"In what fuckin' world is *he* Arnie?"

Frustrated that his joke hadn't landed as expected, Alan responded with arm-waving anger: "The fuckin' Running Man," he yelled. "Fuckin' Schwarzenegger, innit?"

Derek scoffed, walked behind the bar, and poured himself a pint. The barman stared at him in disgust, saying: "You shouldn't be behind here, man."

Derek laughed. "Jog on, Kojak, before I give you a fuckin' hair transplant made outta glass."

The barman cringed and beat a hasty retreat to the safety of the back office. Alan rolled his eyes and shook his head.

"Can't you go a minute without intimidating some poor bastard?"

"If people stop getting in me face, I'll stop threatening them, like," Derek replied. "Frankly, that mardy bald cunt's due a beating. So he might wanna stay in his little hidey-hole."

Alan took a seat beside Mary and patted his shoulder like he was a close friend. "Why'd you run, fella?"

Mary shivered at his touch. "I was frightened."

Alan nodded. "You know how I feel about runners, don'tcha?"

"I know, but I thought I could get your money back."

"And did you?"

Mary squirmed beneath Alan's intense gaze. "A little bit. Not enough."

"How much is not enough?"

"Two hundred and fifty."

Alan drew in a sharp breath and held it. Then he exhaled long and slow. "That takes care of *one* payment, Mary. One fuckin' payment. And you owe five."

"I'm really sorry."

"You can keep your apology, coz I can't fuckin' spend it. And if you were really sorry, you wouldn't have done a runner in the first place. So where's the money?"

"I don't have it with me."

Alan sat back and cold-eyed the quivering man. "This just gets better."

"Swear down, I can get it outta the machine down the road."

"And have you run again? No thanks."

"I wouldn't…"

"I know you wouldn't, coz you're not leaving this table, gadge. Now empty your pockets."

Mary put the contents of his pockets on the table. Thirty pounds in notes, another five in coins, keys, and assorted receipts and other ragged pieces of paper, and a debit card. Alan scooped everything off the table and into his lap.

"Now gimme the PIN number."

Mary stuttered his details.

Alan cocked his head in Derek's direction and waved the card in the air. "Get that two-fifty outta the machine, then come back here."

Pretending not to hear, Derek remained behind the bar and sipped his pint.

Alan's stare intensified. "Ow, I told you to do summat."

Derek smiled. "I know what you said, like. Try a please in there and I might feel like doing it."

Gordy moved towards the bar.

Derek vaulted over the counter and grabbed the man by the throat. He wrapped his other hand around Gordy's wrist and squeezed it to prevent him from struggling. "Feeling brave, fat lad?"

The thug tried to prise Derek's hand from his neck, but as he started choking, he panicked and croaked at his boss for some help.

Mary wondered if it might be possible to use the chaos to make a break for it. Piper must have sensed the moment of opportunity because he put his hand on the man's shoulder and squeezed as he turned towards Eric. "Can't you put a leash on your brother?"

"What makes you think *I've* got any control over him?"

"I'm serious."

"So am I," Eric replied. "Mebbe try being polite for once in your life."

The loan shark rolled his eyes. "Please can you do as I fuckin' asked? *Please?*"

Derek let go of Gordy, who staggered back and gasped for breath. "Well, since you asked so nicely, like," he replied and snatched the card out of Alan's hand.

Gordy rubbed his throat and coughed in a manner that suggested he was trying to get his boss' sympathy. "You got lucky."

Derek grinned. "I'll always get lucky with you, Gord," he said, then fluttered the card in front of Piper's face. "Where's the nearest machine?"

"There's one on Linthorpe Road, about five minutes away."

Derek stormed out and slammed the door. Bottles and glasses shook. Alan directed his hard green gaze at Eric. "You two need a fuckin' attitude adjustment, and fast. You might wanna remember who you're working for. But, you know, you can just keep clowning around if you don't fancy being on me payroll. Mebbe try your fuckin' comedy routine down the benefits office — see what that gets you?"

Eric rubbed his chin and stared into the distance. It was obvious to Mary that he was deciding on whether or not to tell the boss to go fuck himself. His silence suggested he'd keep his thoughts to himself for now.

Piper refocused his attention on Mary. "Now I'm gonna tell you how this shit's gonna go. Gordy's gonna break summat. Your choice. Mebbe an arm, mebbe a leg, but summat's getting broken."

"Please…"

"Please has gone the way of the Dodo. Please disappeared the moment you decided to go all Running Man on me. All things considered, you should thank your lucky fuckin' stars I don't have Gordy press a hot iron to the soles of your feet."

Mary's hand shook as he lifted the pint glass to his face. He spilled more than he drank before placing the drink back on the table. He thought hard about what he could afford to lose. He needed his hands for poker. "My leg," he replied after a long pause.

"Which one?"

"The left."

Alan stood up. "Lie on the floor."

Mary's heart thumped. Dots swarmed like flies before his eyes, and for a second he thought he might faint, but the moment passed and he managed to get on the floor with some dignity.

Mary looked at Alan with imploring eyes, eager to follow orders but also terrified of what was coming. His teeth chattered noisily.

Alan beckoned Gordy forward. The big man came to his side with a grin — finally there was something interesting for him to do.

"Drag him to those steps."

In the right corner, at the rear of the pub, was a small raised seating area. Occasionally, it was used as an impromptu bandstand for small three- and four-piece bands. Three small steps separated the area from the rest of the pub.

Gordy dragged Mary across the floor, his feet scuffing the boards, to the steps. Then he placed Mary in a position that meant his lower leg rested between the top and middle steps.

Alan watched from the bar. "You might wanna chew on summat, Mary."

Eric grabbed several bar mats and carried them over. Mary took them with trembling hands. Eric leaned in close, whispering: "Bite down hard."

Alan sneered as Eric walked towards the front of the bar. "Don't fancy watching?"

"Not really. Seen one broken bone you've seen 'em all."

"You're too fuckin' soft, mate."

"Just 'cause I don't wanna watch Gordy get his rocks off by breaking this poor bastard's leg doesn't mean I'm soft."

Gordy let out a rasping chuckle. "Fuckin' fanny."

Eric sat down. "Sticks and stones, you tubby fucknut."

"You should make him watch," Gordy said. "Man him the fuck up."

Alan bristled at being told what to do. "When did you take charge, Gord?"

"Soz boss, I just…"

"You just overstepped your bounds is what you did."

"Soz boss, I…"

"You need to shut the fuck up now."

Gordy shuffled his shoulders and appeared suitably humbled by looking at the ground with a hangdog expression. Alan clicked his fingers to get his underling's attention. Gordy lifted his head and gave Alan his full attention.

"Do it."

Mary let out a muffled cry of fear as Gordy's rubber-soled feet squeaked along the floorboards and turned his head away at the moment of impact. The pain was like nothing else he'd ever felt, not even his beating by Hilda's Boys came close (mostly because he was unconscious through most of it). Mary bit into the beer mats as he squealed. Then there was another duller crunch as Gordy stomped his leg again. The sharp burst of agony made the previous pain seem like an appetiser. Mary's scream made Alan cringe. He yelled at Gordy to stop.

"The fuckin' bone's poking through, dickhead."

"Soz boss."

"I said *break* his leg," Alan replied. "Not snap the fuckin' thing in half."

"It were an accident, boss."

"Accident? I didn't realise you weren't in control of your motor functions. Lemme get this straight; you're saying that second stamp were a fuckin' mistake?"

"Overzealous, weren't I?"

Spots danced in front of Mary's eyes. The world went in and out of focus. A fresh twinge from the injury kept him from fainting.

While Alan and Gordy bickered, Eric crouched beside him and checked the wound. Mary took his first look at the damage and let out a terrified screech. Sharp jagged bone poked through his calf muscle and tore a hole in the back of his jeans, which were soaked through with blood.

Eric removed the belt from Mary's waist and tied a tight knot in the bulge of calf muscle just below the knee. He cried out again. The blood flow became a trickle.

Gordy smirked. "If it isn't Annie Nightingale?"

Eric shook his head. "It's Florence Nightingale, you silly fat twat."

"What were that?"

"Annie Nightingale's a DJ. If you weren't such a fuckin' moron, you'd know that."

Gordy tugged at Alan's shoulder. "He called us fat, boss."

Piper shrugged him off nonchalantly and brushed at the area where he'd been manhandled. "He's got a point like. The fact you're more concerned about being called fat rather than retarded has me worried."

Gordy frowned. "He called me a moron, not a retard."

"*I'm* calling you a fuckin' retard. Got a problem with that?"

The big man shook his head.

Derek came through the door with the money, stopped, and stared at the mess. "Thought you were only gonna *break* his leg?"

"Gordy decided to put his entire weight on it," Eric replied.

"That's a lotta weight."

"This is muscle not fat," Gordy snapped.

Alan clicked his fingers in frustration. "Enough quips. Where's me money?"

Derek smirked at him with barely disguised contempt. "Where's the magic word?"

"Just gimme the money. I'm in no fuckin' mood…"

"Then make some magic happen."

Alan sighed. "*Please* gimme the fuckin' money, I'm…"

Derek tossed the paper at his boss. Alan didn't bother trying to catch it. Instead, he let the money bounce off his chest and scatter across the floor. He clicked his fingers at Gordy, who eagerly scooped it off the ground and bundled it into his boss' open palm.

Derek laughed. "D'you wipe his arse for him too when he tells ya, Gord?"

Gordy blushed slightly and backed away.

Eric crouched and pressed his hand against Mary's shoulder in an attempt to control his trembling. "Don't be giving him ideas."

Alan wasn't amused. "I swear down, youse two fuckwits are a wisecrack away from unemployment," he said. When he realised how much Mary was shaking, Alan's frown became a grimace. "He's not dying, is he?"

Eric shook his head. "He's in shock."

Alan nodded, snapped his fingers at Gordy, and pointed at the exit. "Let's go."

Then he pointed at the mess. "Get this shite cleaned up and get him outta here before calling an ambulance."

Alan breezed out of the place with Gordy tagging behind in the manner of a loyal service dog.

Eric looked at his brother. "Let's get him outside."

Derek shouted to the barman to grab his mop and bucket and a fuckload of bleach, then he walked over to his brother and brushed him aside. "Just get the fuckin' doors."

Derek grabbed Mary and heaved him off the ground in a fireman's lift. A fresh burst of agony fried his brain to such a degree that he passed out. When he came to, Mary had been placed beside a deep pothole in the car park at the rear of the pub. He tried to scream again, but Eric placed a hand over his mouth.

"I'm gonna phone an ambulance. It should be with you in about twenty minutes. My advice is forget what happened. You tripped over a pothole, or summat. Get me? If you try and snitch to the pigs, Gordy'll come back and finish the job. That's a whole heap of shit you *don't* need."

He removed the hand.

Mary nodded, lay back and shivered violently. It wasn't a cold day, but there was a chill that went deep into his bones. He wondered if this was his body going into shock. He started crying softly.

Eric grasped his shoulder, squeezed, and told him not to worry. Then he got up, brushed down his jeans, and walked away without looking back.

Before the stress and trauma knocked him out cold, Mary wondered if this was as bad as life was going to get.

He was wrong about that.

Life was going to get a hell of a lot worse.

2.

IT TOOK the ambulance longer than anticipated to arrive. More than an hour passed before Mary was loaded into an ambulance and taken for an operation. Infection set in the leg, which when combined with the catastrophic damage inflicted by Gordy, meant that after several operations the situation was so severe that the surgeons had to amputate. This was followed by another coma, and a slow, painful recovery. The only benefit was he got his own room, even if he was too unwell to really enjoy the solitude.

It also brought him a lot of visitors — welcome *and* unwelcome.

Early during his hospital stay, well outside hospital visiting hours, Jezza slinked into the far corner of the room and stared at him with tear-glazed eyes. Even by his usual standards, the junky was pale and gaunt. His clothes hung off his stick-thin frame, and his cheekbones were as sharp as blades. The wild mop of dark hair on his head made it look like he'd been dragged through a hedge backwards. Something other than the habit was eating away at him. Mary waved at his friend and whispered a faint hello, before adding that he wasn't supposed to have visitors. Jezza chewed his fingernails before returning a forced smile.

"I'm sorry man," Jezza replied.

"You didn't... break my leg."

"I know that man, but I'm sorry just the same," he added. "I didn't know it was gonna go down like this."

"I dunno... what you mean."

"Shit, bruv, they've proper fucked you up," he added. "I didn't know they was gonna mess you up like this."

"What... are you saying?"

Jezza looked around like they were being spied upon, stepped out of the shadows in the corner of the room, and moved closer to the bed. "I told them where you was."

Cold realisation gripped Mary: all this horror had been piled on him by a man he considered a friend. They'd shared conversations, meals, booze, and told each other secrets that would otherwise have remained hidden. Mary had helped his friend when he was at rock bottom, and this was how he'd been repaid. He wondered how much the junky had been given for his betrayal, and suspected it was a lot less than thirty pieces of silver. "I hope… it was worth it," he said bitterly.

"I'm sorry, man. I was desperate. I needed a fix."

Tears formed at the corners of Mary's eyes, which he wiped away with a bed sheet. He just about managed to keep his calm. "If you'd needed cash… you could've come to me, you know."

The junky cringed with shame.

"How much did Alan pay you?"

Jezza shook his head. "No point raking over old coals now. I just want you to know I'm sorry, bruv."

"I wanna know," Mary insisted. "You owe me *that* much."

"Fifty," he replied in a barely audible whisper.

Mary looked down at the space where his left leg used to be and began to cry. All this mess and pain for a few hits of heroin. He wondered if this was his lot in life, to accept his pain and humiliation without fighting back. He wanted to scream in Jezza's face, but instead wiped his eyes and, with a calm voice, said: "Get out. Don't come back."

The junky opened the door and slipped through it.

As soon as he was alone, Mary broke down into screaming hysterics that the nurses eventually had to subdue with tranquilisers.

A couple of days later, Mary awakened with Raffles at the foot of his bed. "How're you doing, mate?"

"I've been better."

"I can imagine."

"Actually, unless you've had your leg snapped by a fuckin' gorilla, I'm not sure you *can* imagine it."

"Soz, mate, poor choice of words."

"I'm sorry, it's not…"

"Stop apologising," Raffles replied, standing up. "It was a stupid thing to say. How the fuck could I know what you've been through?"

The junky was tall and lean. With a few extra pounds and a bit more colour in his cheeks, he would probably be considered good looking. His appearance wasn't helped by short, ragged hair that he'd cut himself and dirty, sallow skin. He still had a pleasant smile, even though his teeth were starting to yellow, that he flashed for his friend. "I came here to let you know that when you get out, you've always got a place to stay."

Mary let out a sigh. "For a second, I thought you were gonna tell me you'd sold me out, too."

Raffles' dark eyes narrowed. "Meaning what, exactly?"

Realising his mistake, Mary smiled and shook his head. "Forget it."

"Bullshit. You can't drop summat like that into a conversation and expect me to act like it never got said. Who sold you out?"

Mary's face twitched as he fought back tears. "Jezza."

"How?"

Mary's heart pounded against his ribcage. The fear coursing through his veins wasn't about revealing what Jezza had done to him, it was the dread of how his friend was going to react. Raffles was angry at the best of times, so this might tip him over the edge into the kind of rage that could have serious consequences.

"He told Piper where to find me."

The junky gritted his teeth and his hands formed fists that he tapped against his upper thighs. "For how much?"

"I don't…"

"How much?"

"Fifty."

"You're saying to me that Jezza had you crippled for a couple of fixes?"

"He didn't…"

"Didn't what? Cripple you? It might've been Gordy who snapped your leg on Piper's say so, but it was Jez who put you in the frame. He might as well have done the deed himself. Oh, that bastard's gotta go, mate. I'm gonna fix that prick."

"I know you mean well, Raff, but that's not gonna change owt," he said. "You know summat, I just wanna put all this behind me."

Raffles leaned forward with the air of someone who couldn't believe what had just been said. "Behind you? Are you kidding me?" he snapped. "Mate, you've got months of fuckin' physio ahead, getting used to walking again on a false leg, and you wanna put what they did behind you? Fuck that shit. These bastards have gotta pay."

"And once they've paid — will that bring my leg back?"

Raffles moved back and forth along the width of the room. "What's that gotta do with owt?"

"Have you ever heard the saying, 'an eye for an eye leaves the whole world blind'?"

"Fuck off! The dickhead who said that didn't have some fuckin' fat boy using their leg as a balance beam."

"I don't want any of this — none of it — and I don't think I deserve it, but now that it's here, I can either accept what's happening or I can rot with rage. I'd rather move on."

Raffles wore an expression of disgust. "Every shitty thing that's happened to you — the face, the wife, the house, and now the leg — you always just accept it, and act like it's *your* fault. For once, whyn't you just fuckin' kick off and take it out on some cunt? Gordy Willis, for starters. Even *you've* gotta accept that that lardy prick needs to take a fuckin' blade."

Mary accepted that Gordy was an awful human being, and what he did deserved punishment. Unfortunately, they lived in a world where the bad rarely received the punishment they deserved; but stabbing Gordy would only leave a gap that would be filled by another horrible person. Even so, Mary suspected that Raffles' rage had less to do with what happened to him, and more to do with his own experience at the hands of Gordy.

Back when he'd been a regular working man, Raffles had got into some financial difficulties, forcing him to take what he believed was going to be nothing more than a short-term loan from Alan Piper. But as these things have a tendency to do, his problems got worse, meaning he couldn't make the payments. He tried juggling his bills, and moved his money around with the dexterity of a card shuffler, but even so he wasn't able to make good what he owed. Initially, Piper showed him some degree of sympathy. However, this consideration only lasted as long as he considered Raffles (or Darren Mulherne as he was back then) someone capable of settling his debts. It took a few weeks, but eventually Piper's patience ran out and he sent his pet gorilla Gordy to either get the money or spill some blood. Gordy broke both of Raffles' arms and dumped him in a bin behind a local pub and closed the lid, knowing that his damaged limbs ensured he wouldn't be able to climb back out.

Shit like that can scar a man.

Mary didn't say any of these things to his friend. Instead, he sat and listened as Raffles tried to convince him to take revenge on Gordy and Piper. He extended him the same courtesy when he returned the next day and the day after. He listened until the ravings of an angry man started to take on the patina of reasoned argument. Still, he probably wouldn't have considered the possibility of revenge if a couple of unwanted visitors hadn't shown up at the foot of his bed a few days later.

Mary woke up from a horrible nightmare to find Alan Piper sitting on the visitor's chair with Gordy Willis standing beside him. He blinked and rubbed his eyes in disbelief, still wondering if this was a dream. Piper was as handsome and suave as ever, with his flawless haircut, high cheekbones, and immaculately tailored suit, and Gordy still looked like a shaved gorilla that had been shrink-wrapped inside some Jacamo threads. It wasn't until Piper spoke that Mary realised it wasn't his imagination.

"We need a word."

He sat up in bed and reached for the call button.

"Get that *bastard* outta this room."

Gordy tensed up. "Ow, looka…"

Sensing things were going to explode, Piper gestured for the big man to leave, but Gordy refused to move. Meanwhile, Mary's finger rested on the alert button. "I'm serious."

Piper turned towards his underling, snarling: "When I tell you to leave, you fuckin' *leave*."

Gordy tried to argue with his boss that it was probably better for everyone that he remained in the room, but Piper was having none of it. "It's not up for discussion. You've caused enough fuckin' trouble as it is. Gerrout Gordy."

The big man cast a savage glance at Mary, the kind that suggests later violence, and took his time fussing and fidgeting over things in his pockets as a delaying tactic. This worked until Piper lost his patience and yelled at him to get the fuck out, at which point Gordy lowered his head and shuffled out of the room in a suitably humbled manner.

Piper turned his attention back to Mary. For once, he wasn't smirking; he was wearing his serious face for serious business.

"I'm sorry you lost your leg," he said. "Gordy went too far."

"Too far?" Mary replied incredulously. "I nearly died thanks to you."

"It was Gordy that broke your leg."

"On *your* orders."

Piper's otherwise impassive face twitched. "If you'd paid your debt in the first place none of this would've happened."

"So it's *my* fault?"

"I didn't say that, but if you wanna get into it, then yeah, if you'd paid your bill on time then there would've been no need for any of this shite. That being said, Gordy was outta control. He was only supposed to break your leg, not snap the fuckin' thing, so I wanna apologise for that."

"That's big of you."

There was another flutter of irritation, as Piper realised his magnanimous moment wasn't going quite as well as he'd hoped. "I came here to offer a gesture of goodwill," he said.

The way Piper had twisted the narrative infuriated Mary. Somehow, the loan shark was now the innocent victim in all this, caught between Mary's reluctance to repay his debt and Gordy's stupidity. Blameless.

For the first time, Raffles' suggestion of revenge seemed almost comforting.

"You said summat about goodwill."

"I came here to cancel half your debt."

Mary sniggered in disbelief. "*Half?*"

"Gordy shoulda broke your leg, not fucked it forever. So that shit's on me. But you shouldn't have run, so that one's on *you*. Judging by the fact that I've not had the pigs busting down me door, I figure you kept your mouth shut. But you've become a bit of a cautionary tale out there on the grapevine — every fucker's paying on time. Nobody wants to end up like you."

A shiver of rage passed through him. "My fuckin' life's over," he snapped. "But I'm glad you got a cautionary tale out of it."

"And you've had your debt cut in two."

"Fuck you."

A moment of fury had Piper out of his chair. He stopped himself from storming towards the bed and instead made fists that he stuffed in his trouser pockets. "You're lucky I know it's just the anger talking, or I'd be bringing Gordy back in to take the *other* leg."

"How am I supposed to pay you back?"

Alan jammed his fists deeper. "I'm not a complete bastard," he said. "Once you're back on your feet *then* we'll talk."

"My *foot*, you mean?"

Piper's upper lip curled briefly, before it became a humourless grin, and he turned away, shaking his head in disgust. It was obvious that he'd expected his gesture to be welcomed with complete gratitude. He wasn't happy that his visit hadn't gone the way he'd anticipated.

The Alan Pipers of this world always get away clean, Mary thought. Maybe it was time for him to suffer some pain, to face the consequences of his actions. Mary made a mental note to get in touch with Raffles and find out if his friend was serious about revenge.

"I'm not expecting you to be grateful," Piper said. "But you might wanna keep those wisecracks on the downlow. Otherwise, I'll leave you to have a private conversation with Gordy. You can see what that'll bring you. We clear?"

It took everything Mary had to control his fury. He kept a straight face and a neutral tone. "As crystal," he replied.

Piper primped his hair with a well-manicured hand. "Then look after yourself."

The loan shark exited the room and closed the door behind him. As soon as he heard Piper's feet clacking down the corridor, Mary's composure deserted him and he let everything go in one convulsive sob. Tears streamed down his cheeks. His body shook with a poisonous mixture of outrage and regret. He cried himself to sleep with several thoughts running through his head on a continuous comforting loop.

Get strong, walk again, get revenge. Get strong, walk again, get revenge. Get strong, walk again, get revenge.

3.

WEEKS PASSED into months. Mary's hate intensified and crystallised, and his mind focused on three main tasks. He wanted to walk and run without a limp on a prosthetic leg; his finances needed fixing; and he needed a solid plan to get revenge on Alan Piper and Gordy Willis.

When he wasn't working with his physiotherapist, Mary hit the gym on a daily basis, building muscle, strength, and stamina. He quit booze, ate healthily, and supplemented his diet with protein powders and Creatine.

Mary's new lifestyle was funded by an unbreakable winning streak. He started pulling in over two hundred a night playing on-line poker. However, when the conditions were right, he made between five hundred and a thousand quid a day. Over the course of six months, Mary won more than forty grand.

Eager to see if his luck extended to the real world, he visited local Poker games again. He never risked anything larger than his stake money, and told himself that once it was gone, he would call it a night. But Mary never left a game empty-handed.

Cards fell in his favour. Even when the hand was weak, Mary's bluff wasn't. His smirking confidence overwhelmed even the strongest opponents. Experienced players began to doubt themselves in Mary's presence and played good hands badly or left the table when it would have been smarter to stick around. He became unbeatable. And at the end of the evening, when he walked away from the table with a fat wad of cash, Mary made sure to accentuate his limp. It was all part of the plan.

All the while, he paid Alan Piper the bare minimum, even missing the occasional payment because it irritated the loan shark so much. The thing that infuriated him most was the knowledge that Mary could now afford to pay off the debt in one chunk.

Even though it was costing him a small fortune in interest, Mary continued dragging out the process of paying off his debt, because it gave him the time he needed to get used to walking and running on the prosthetic. Mary often trained until the flesh of his stump was raw and he was so exhausted that he could barely lift his limbs.

On the day that he walked out of physiotherapy without a hint of a limp, Mary went to Stewart Park, sat on a bench near the Captain Cook Museum, and placed a call to Raffles. He said only two words, but his friend understood exactly what Mary meant when he said:

"I'm ready."

He wasn't, but he said it anyway.

4.

DARREN 'RAFFLES' Mulherne watched Piper's gate through a pair of binoculars. There was a slight smile on his gaunt face that slowly turned into a grin. Mary wondered what was making him so happy. From his position, behind a dense thicket of trees, he saw a distant figure that could have been Gordy Willis bent over in front of the entry pad. The gate opened with a shudder and the big man got in a small blue car and drove into the estate. Then the gate juddered closed.

This was the first time Raffles had smiled over the past couple of days. Mary was eager to find out what had made him so happy.

"What's the dealio?"

Raffles lowered the glasses. "Fat boy didn't cover the display when he typed in the numbers. He tapped four times. Two from the top, one from the second, and one from the third row. I'm figuring he typed in Piper's birthday, so I reckon the third number is six, coz Piper's older than us but he's not *that* fuckin' old. Meaning the final number is either seven, eight, or nine. And the first two digits are one, two, or three."

Mary couldn't help but feel a little disappointed. Judging by the grin, he'd expected Raffles to have broken the code. "That's not quite Alan Turing, is it?"

"Ow, you cheeky cunt, I don't see *you* going all Enigma on this shit," he snapped. "Besides, I haven't finished working me magic yet."

It took several phone calls and a couple of favours to get the information he needed. "It's the twenty-third of February, nineteen sixty-seven."

"How the hell di…"

"Ask and ye shall receive," he said with a shrug. "I've done some favours over the years. Figure now's as good a time as any to call them in."

"So what's the plan?"

"We follow the fat lad home, and take him out first."

"Why?"

"Coz he's devoted, that's why. If we get Piper first, Gordy'll never stop hunting us down. He'll cripple *everybody* in his boss' little black book. And considering you're also on the list, he'll probably take your other leg."

The memory of Gordy slamming his foot down made Mary shudder. There was a fleeting phantom pain where his lower leg used to be. He closed his eyes and conjured happy thoughts until the moment passed.

Raffles frowned. "You okay, mate?"

Mary nodded. "Just reliving the moment."

"I promise you they're gonna suffer."

"What about Gordy? Won't Piper look for *his* killer?"

"He's too fuckin' selfish for that. That'll involve actually giving a fuck. Besides, if we do them both on the same day, we'll probably be in the clear. *Everybody* hates Piper. Even his wife despises him. That's a lotta potential suspects for the pigs to wade through. Chances are they'll come up short. We've just gotta hold our nerve."

They waited in a lay-by until Gordy drove past, and followed him for the rest of the day. There were several long dull hours of watching the big man visit various homes and businesses. He went in with a scowl and exited with a smile, which meant people either paid up quickly, or they got caught on the business end of his fists. As soon as it got dark, Gordy ended his shift and drove home to a small terrace in Grangetown. Mary had expected something less ordinary, possibly a dank cave decorated with skulls and swastikas, so the realisation that the man lived in a regular home made him wonder momentarily if they were doing the right thing. Gordy crouched in front of a small planter beside his front door and stroked the petals of a red flower. Something about this private moment gave Mary pause for thought. He kept the notion to himself, but it made him feel unsettled.

As soon as their target was in the house, Raffles grunted and started the car. "We'll hit him later tonight."

His discomfort intensified. "What happened to killing them both on the same day?"

Raffles shrugged. "He's holding Piper's money."

"You don't need it."

"You're right, I *don't* need it, but I wannit just the same."

"But...."

"But nothing. You know me. Or you should by now. When I stole from that church raffle, the money was secondary. I wanted the *thrill*. I wanted to see all those disappointed Christian faces. Fuck them, and their God. And fuck him, *and* his boss."

5.

IT WAS past midnight when they returned. Raffles parked beneath a broken light a couple of streets away from Gordy's place. They waited in the car until the area was quiet. They watched a couple of loud drunks stagger past and didn't move until their voices faded from earshot. Then they walked briskly towards the house, making sure they stayed in the shadows. Neither man spoke. In fact, they hadn't made a sound in over an hour. Words were unnecessary because they'd discussed the plan repeatedly over takeaway pizza earlier in the evening. Raffles would bring their target to the door, give him a couple of blows to the gut, push him inside, and then Mary would deliver the coup de grâce.

They looked up and down the street, which was clear of people, and gave the house a glance. The living room light was on. A big silhouette appeared behind the pale curtains, waited a moment, and finally moved away. Mary's breath caught in his chest and stayed there until his brain pleaded with him to exhale. Raffles pounded the door with his knuckles as Mary waited off to the side and hyperventilated. He'd waited months for this moment, relishing the thought of getting revenge, of ending Gordy's life, but now that it had arrived, he wasn't sure it was what he wanted. Surely there was a better way than this.

"Come on out, you fat prick."

The door yanked open and Gordy stepped out. "What the fuck did you just say, junky?"

Mary tried to call it off, but only managed a hoarse whisper that became a choking cough. This distraction was enough to get the big man to turn his head. Raffles used it to his advantage, got in close, and plunged a meat knife deep into his opponent's gut. Gordy grunted in pain and surprise and pushed his attacker away. He tried to get back into the house, but Raffles buried the weapon in his side. Mary expected it to be cinematic, with carefully choreographed violence and theatrical shrieks of pain, but the tangle between the pair was clumsy and relatively noiseless. As his friend got ready to use the blade again, the big man surprised him with a hard right hook that put him on his arse. Gordy stumbled through the front door and tried to close it, but Mary threw his weight against it, and the momentum sent both men tumbling into the hallway. Gordy's attempt to get off the ground ended when his hands repeatedly slid through the blood on the laminate. Eventually, he gave up, lay back, and slowly blinked in shock as a pool of claret formed around him. Gordy lifted his hand with difficulty and pointed at something to Mary's right. On a storage unit strewn with knick-knacks and keys was a miniature shrine in two halves of a presentation box. In the right-hand half was a collage of photos of a woman at various stages of her life. To the left was a small patchwork teddy bear assembled from various materials. Mary had seen something similar at a friend's funeral. The family were presented with small bears made from the clothes of the deceased as they left the venue.

He handed the thing to Gordy, who cuddled it against his neck and closed his eyes. He was still breathing, but everything was starting to slow. There was no pleasure in watching this man-child hug his mother's effigy. The only feeling he had was one of sadness.

"What the fuck're you doing?" Raffles snapped. "Why'd you give him *that* thing?"

"Coz he asked for it."

"Are you soft in the head, or summat?"

"What's it matter to you?"

"He doesn't deserve it."

Raffles moved forward as if to snatch the item from the big man's grasp. Mary rested his hand on his friend's chest and shook his head. "Leave it. He's finished."

"After what he did to you? No, mate, he doesn't deserve any kindness."

"You're right, he did do it to *me*. And I'm saying leave it."

Raffles glared at the dying man.

Mary gave his chest a gentle push. "Go and find the money you were after."

The junky went into the living room and immediately began pulling it apart. Gordy gave the bear one final hug, then his face went slack, and he pissed himself. After a few seconds there was also the unmistakable whiff of shit.

There was no relief, nor any catharsis, for Mary, only an increasing belief that he'd made the wrong decision.

Raffles emerged holding a plastic bag of cash, along with a rag and a jug of water. "Bingo."

"What's the jug for?"

"Cleaning evidence."

"How much is in the bag?"

"About six grand."

Raffles sniffed the air and wrinkled his nose. "He's gone?"

Mary nodded.

Raffles reached down as if to pluck the bear from the dead man's grasp, but Mary grabbed him and pinned him against the wall. The junky seemed shocked at his friend's reaction. "Why the fuck do you care what I take?"

"I just do."

"Fuck it. Fine. He can keep it. It's a raggedy piece of shite, anyway."

As they left the house, Raffles wiped away blood splashes from the door and poured water over the spatters on the paving stones until they were so diluted that they were pretty much invisible. Then he locked the door and walked to Gordy's car.

"What are you doing?"

"What the fuck's it look like?"

"Why're we taking his car?"

"In case someone turns up," Raffles replied. "If there's no car, they're gonna assume he's not home."

The confident way with which Raffles had dispatched Gordy made Mary wonder if his friend had done this kind of thing before. "You seem to know whatcha doing."

He shrugged. "Used to work for Billy Chin, didn't I? You gotta multitask when you're in his crew. Slackers in't gonna get very far with a slave driver like Billy. And just being a thief in't gonna cut it. If you can't carry your weight, then as far as he's concerned you're *dead* fuckin' weight, and he'll cut you loose. If you wanna graft for the Junky King, you've gotta be cool with the rough stuff. Know what I mean?"

Mary nodded like he understood, but he didn't. Nothing would ever make him feel okay with what they were doing. As much as he despised Gordy, there was no emotional release in being part of his murder and watching him die. The overwhelming sensation he had was emptiness tinged with despair. But he didn't voice any of this, or question if hitting Piper was the right thing, instead he patted his friend on the shoulder and said: "I get what you're saying, mate."

6.

RAFFLES VISITED Gordy's place several times over the course of the day, watching for signs of trouble. When he returned home, he told Mary that they were in the clear. Some thug that Raffles didn't recognise went to the door a couple of times, but he never waited around long enough for a response. He knocked, stood on the step for five seconds, then got back in his car and drove away.

The junky rolled a fat joint, passed it to Mary and asked him if was prepared to go through with killing Piper.

He wasn't, but he exhaled and nodded. "I'm ready."

Raffles squinted through a haze of foul smelling smoke. "Ready like you were with Gordy?"

"I dunno what happened there."

The junky took back the spliff and sucked up a big lungful. "You got scared," he said. "That's what happened."

Mary took a hit and let it out. When he passed the spliff back, Raffles shook his head and told him to take another drag.

"Why?"

"Dutch courage," Raffles replied.

"I thought that was gin?"

"Yeah, mebbe. However, that shit in your hand is Amsterdam's finest. Gin just gets you pissed, but what's in your lungs right now will numb you the fuck out. And you're gonna need to be desensitised to take care of Piper. Coz I'm not gonna do it on my own this time. You hear me?"

The weed hit Mary hard, turned down the volume in his head, and made him feel like a dispassionate observer of his own pain and misery. It wasn't that his concerns were gone, because they weren't, but they weren't bothering him anymore. Even the thought of dealing with Piper didn't faze him. So he wasn't lying when he promised he was ready.

The look Raffles gave him was one of suspicion. "I'll believe that shit when I see it."

Once it was dark, they drove back to the loan shark's estate, returned to their previous hiding spot, and waited. As soon as the passing traffic thinned out, they pulled on balaclavas and crossed the road. Raffles typed the code in the keypad and patted his friend's shoulder when the gate opened. He jammed a wedge underneath it to ensure that it couldn't close, then grabbed Mary by the arm and led him up the path. They stayed in the shadows, away from the security cameras, using the darkness to disguise their approach to the front steps of the house.

Raffles plucked a small stone from the driveway and heaved it at one of the living room windows. It bounced off the pane and cracked the glass. Piper snatched open the curtains and frowned at the damage. He muttered continuously and looked around for signs of trouble. Because Raffles and Mary were crouched out of view, Piper couldn't see anything untoward, so he drew the curtains again. A few seconds later, the front door opened.

They were in the shadows on either side of the steps as Piper rushed down to the drive and moved towards the window. "What the fuck?" he muttered, unable to understand why this had happened.

Raffles came out of his crouch first. Mary hesitated because the effects of the weed had worn off and he was troubled by the thought of another murder. Raffles took a couple of steps and swung the blade. The crunch of his feet on gravel alerted the loan shark, who turned his body to avoid the attack. The blade struck his left shoulder. Piper hollered in pain and threw a wild right that caught Raffles chin and had him wobbling like a drunkard.

Piper turned and almost ran straight into Mary. An idiotic expression of shock made his handsome face ugly for a moment. Mary pushed the knife into his chest, but when the knife struck bone and resistance he hesitated long enough to allow Piper to push him away. Instead of going back into the house, the loan shark panicked and ran in the direction of the lawn.

"Don't let him get to the woods," Raffles yelled as he brushed his buddy aside.

Mary picked up the pace as best he could, but his stump was sweating and the prosthetic leg felt unstable. Raffles caught Piper as he reached the grass and jabbed him in the side. The loan shark kept running until he reached an industrial sized sprinkler that was turning the lawn into a lagoon. Raffles slid along the slippery turf, skidded as his feet tried to get purchase, and landed on his back. For some reason, Piper rounded the sprinkler, came back, and decided to plough one of his slippered feet into the junky's midsection. Raffles slashed out and sliced his attacker across the abdomen. Piper grunted and almost ran into Mary, who made a half-hearted slash that missed its target by a good couple of feet.

"Don't tickle the cunt," Raffles yelled. "Fuckin' kill him."

Piper shrieked and took off again. The junky managed to get upright and block his exit. The loan shark dodged his attackers and made another break for the trees. Mary gave chase and swiped his knife through the air. His heart was no longer in it, he wanted to be anywhere but here, so he put himself between Piper and his friend to cover the injured man's escape, occasionally swishing his knife around convincingly to make it look like he was following the plan. Raffles bellowed encouragement and tried to sprint to the front. That was when Mary decided to take a dive. He let his false leg catch in the slick turf and went sprawling on his belly. Unable to alter his stride, Raffles tripped over his friend's trailing leg and slid across the lawn.

Piper ran in the direction of the exit, but his progress was slow. A sense of relief washed over Mary that he wouldn't be involved in yet another death. This brief moment of elation turned to terror when he noticed the Stanton brothers watching everything with frowned expressions of bemusement. Piper let out a howl of delight and screamed for help.

Derek Stanton went around his boss and rushed towards Raffles. The moment his feet hit the wet grass the big man went into a slide that put him on his arse within swinging distance. The junky lashed out and opened a deep gash along Derek's left shoulder. He yelled in pain, landed a right hook that made the Raffles wobble, grabbed his knife hand and squeezed it until he dropped the blade.

Then he kept squeezing until the bones in the junky's hand went snap, crackle and pop, and his fingers started bending in strange new directions. Raffles squealed for help as he tried to wriggle free of Derek's grasp.

Mary's false leg felt loose, so he kept his hand on it as he got upright. He stumbled towards the two men as they struggled and stabbed Derek in the side. Mary didn't go too deep, because he didn't want to kill the man, but he wanted to hurt him enough to give Raffles the chance to escape.

Derek yelped like an injured dog, pushed Mary away, fell backwards and slid away from trouble. Mary pulled his friend off the ground and dragged him down the gravel path as he sobbed and whimpered about the state of his broken hand.

They cut through the trees and made their way to Gordy's car. Mary bundled his friend into the rear passenger seat and started the car. It had been quite a while since he'd last driven. He tested the clutch and brake pedals with his false leg a few times as Raffles groaned.

"What the fuck're you doing?"

"Trying out the pedals," Mary replied. "False leg, remember?"

"Just drive."

"Where?"

"There's a scalpel wielder who does private work for Billy. Lemme give him a call now."

Mary eased out of the layby, thankful that there wasn't much traffic around, as he got used to the pedals and tried changing gears and braking as much as he could. Sometimes he over- and under-compensated because he couldn't feel the bite point of the clutch and the car jerked in response, but as they reached Guisborough he navigated the roads with confidence. It took some time to find the place because Raffles kept passing out from the pain and Mary didn't know the streets particularly well.

They pulled up on a side street not far from the old Priory, and Mary helped his friend into a small terraced house, up a flight of stairs, and into a spare bedroom that had been turned into an impromptu operating theatre.

A gaunt middle-aged man in dirty scrubs helped get Raffles onto a gurney. Then he folded his arms and frowned. "That looks bad, Raff. Remind me again why I should treat you?"

This confused Mary. "I thought you said this shit was arranged?"

"Did he now?" the man said. "Is this like an arranged marriage? Where some fucker gets the surprise of their life? Coz I phoned Billy after you called, and he doesn't recall you doing any work for him recently. So you need to pay up or get out."

Raffles nodded. "What's the going rate now?"

"A grand."

"You're taking the piss, mate."

"Am I?"

"Billy pays half that."

"Yeah, coz Billy's a mate. So he gets mate's rates. *You*, however, are a cunt. So you get cunt's rates."

"Have a heart, Pen."

"I *do* have a heart," he replied matter-of-factly. "I convinced a very angry Billy not to come here and kill you. I did you the biggest favour you're gonna get today. But my generosity only goes so far. Pay up or get out — the choice is yours."

Raffles reclined in the gurney and hitched his good thumb over his shoulder. "Go get Gordy's bag from the boot. Then grab a gee and come on back."

James Pennington looked concerned. "That wouldn't be Gordy Willis, would it?"

"That's right."

"He's trouble I don't need."

"I wouldn't worry about it."

"Hard not to worry," Pen replied. "If you've got Gordy's money, he's gonna hunt it down. I hope you've got a nice coffin picked out."

"The only body going in a box belongs to that tubby sack of shit. But God help the poor bastards that have to carry it."

Pen refolded his arms. "*You* iced Gordy Willis?"

Raffles gathered his thoughts for a moment before he replied. "I didn't do shit. I just found him that way."

"I find it hard to believe."

"What's hard to believe about it?"

"The whole fucking thing."

"Why's that, then? I mean, somebody was gonna finish off that prick sooner or later. It's not like he was a popular guy."

There was a smirk on the surgeon's face. "That much I get," he said. "What I'm finding really hard to believe is that *somebody* killed Gordy and they *didn't* take the money. Then you come along like Mister Right-Place, Right-Time and just casually find him *and* the money. If you're gonna feed me bullshit like that at least make sure it's convincing."

Raffles dropped the act and smiled. "Do you care about Gordy?"

The surgeon shook his head. "Now that he's dead? No."

"Then yeah, I iced the fat prick," Raffles said. "Now, are you gonna treat me? Or do I need to go someplace else?"

Pen picked up a syringe and fixed a fresh needle onto it. "If your friend gets the money, I'll do whatever you want."

As Mary went back to the car, he had the uneasy sensation that something wasn't right. The speed with which Pen had accepted Gordy's death was the issue. It wouldn't be beyond the realms of possibility for the surgeon to drug Raffles and make phone enquiries about Gordy. Mary opened the boot, left the money undisturbed, and grabbed one of the knives. Then he locked up, took a deep, calming breath, and went back into the house.

PART THREE: TROUBLE

1.

FRENCHY ALLEN stitched the gash on Piper's lower abdomen with the easy confidence of a man who'd sewn up miles of similar wounds over the years. It helped that his patient was unconscious, preventing him from putting the ex-surgeon off his stride with his constant complaints about the quality of the handiwork.

Frenchy's hands were the only deft thing about him. In fact, Frenchy's nickname had more to do with his dietary requirements than any desire to live on the continent. Albert Allen's nickname came from the enormous quantities of French Fries he'd put away over the years. All those carbs had stacked a fair bit of weight on his frame. Twenty-odd stone, in fact, which was a lot of chunk to squeeze into five-feet eight inches. He swiped a hand through his greasy grey hair and cast a glance in my direction. "I think he's done."

I looked up from the dull paperback I was reading and stared at him. "Think or know?"

"Know," he said. "I'll get some dressings on, give him some antibiotics, and leave some painkillers."

I reclined on the fancy leather sofa and left him to finish his work. I dipped back into the book, but quickly lost interest. It had a lot of fancy words. The author seemed to believe that long sentences and obscure references were suitable replacements for story and character. A competent editor would have stolen the author's well-thumbed thesaurus and told him to get to the point.

My phone rang. I'd sent my brother to Gordy's place to do the dirty work of finding out what the man knew about all this business. I wondered for a moment how badly my brother had tortured Gordy, then decided that it didn't matter. The boss wanted names, and it didn't matter how he got them. Even if Gordy was innocent and knew nothing, my brother was likely to hurt him because there was bad blood between them.

"Yeah?"

"Gordy's come to a full stop."

Dead.

"What the hell did you…."

"Whoa, whoa, whoa, Judge Judy, before you start casting excursions, this shit has nowt to do with me. I found him this way. He's been Tobied."

Carved up.

"Any clues?"

"How the fuck would I know?" he replied. "Although there *is* summat strange."

"Go on."

"He's holding a teddy bear."

"A teddy bear?"

If this was street slang, I hadn't heard it before.

"Is that a new drug, or summat?"

"What the fuck're you talking about?" my brother snapped. "A fuckin' teddy bear, like an actual kid's toy. All patchwork and shit."

It seemed odd for someone as brutal and ruthless as Gordy Willis to be willingly holding a child's toy. Was it a sign? Maybe a new gang thing? Or was it something simpler than this. I asked my brother to look around. It didn't take him long to find the answer.

"There's a presentation box on the sideboard," he said. "It shows him next to some old woman. And there's a buncha pics of her when she were younger."

It was some kind of shrine, most likely for Gordy's mum or maybe his grandmother. "This patchwork bear — is it made outta clothing fabric?"

"Yeah, why?"

"Coz if he was drawing to a full stop, he might want summat to comfort him."

A patchwork bear made out of his mother's clothes might be just the sort of thing to help Gordy as he took his last few breaths.

"How badly was he Tobied?"

"Bad enough to finish him."

"Oh, you're funny," I said. "Remind me to laugh sometime."

"Well, I dunno what the fuck you're getting at, do I? Mister vague and fuckin' mysterious."

"What I mean is, how many carvings?"

"Two."

"Where?"

"Front and side."

"Is he on his front or his back?"

"Back."

"Does he look like he moved?"

"Judging by the undisturbed mess around him, no."

"So someone gave him the bear?"

"Yeah, probably."

I ran the scenario through my head. It was an odd thing to do. Why would you hand something comforting to a man you'd just stabbed? Why extend a scumbag like Gordy any shred of sympathy? The only thing I could think of was that it was the same two people. One did the killing, the other did the remorse.

Then I replayed the events of this evening, particularly what happened to my brother. His first injury was the deeper of the two, even though the second attacker had the opportunity to bury his blade to the hilt. My brother bragged that his cat-like reflexes saved him, but anybody ruthless enough would have kebabed his liver and kidneys. No, what saved Derek wasn't his reflexes, but an attacker who didn't want to hurt him badly.

"You're gonna need to order Mr Muscle," I said, meaning a cleaner who specialises in body disposal.

"Way ahead of you," my brother replied.

"Then close up and get back here."

After I hung up, I noticed that Frenchy had Piper's phone pressed against his ear. His frown suggested it wasn't a happy conversation. The moment he realised I was available, Frenchy thrust the phone in my direction.

"You need to take this."

"Who is it?"

"Pen."

I eased off the sofa and grabbed the handset. "Go on."

"Who'm I talking to?"

"Eric."

"Stanton?"

"No, Clapton," I said, adding as the voice sighed. "Yes, fuckin' Stanton."

"The Frenchman tells me that somebody carved up pretty boy this evening."

"That's right."

"I think I might know who."

"Think or know?"

"Well, it depends on how much money pretty boy's offering."

"He's having a post-surgical nap."

"So wake him up with the good news."

I looked at Piper, appearing almost beatific in his tranquilised state. He'd want answers, but I didn't want to be the one to wake him up. He wasn't likely to come out of his slumber in a good mood. I covered the handset and told Frenchy to do the honours. The man muttered under his breath and started hitting Piper's face with soft strikes that got gradually harder.

"I've got a pretty defined price in mind," Pen said. "Five gees."

"You might wanna undefine that figure, coz sure as shite, Alan isn't gonna pay that much."

"Whyn't you let him decide for himself?"

Piper came around gradually, moaning and mumbling, then perked up quickly when Frenchy pressed a tube of smelling salts under his nose. The loan shark blinked then looked down at the crooked line across his abdomen.

"What the fuck is this shit?"

"Surgery scars," Frenchy replied.

"Did you stitch it with your eyes closed, or summat? I look like Frankenfuck."

The surgeon rolled his eyes. "I think you'll find that Frankenfuck was the doctor."

"You might wanna watch that tone with me, Frenchy. Otherwise...."

I thrust the handset under my boss' nose and said: "As amusing as this lovers' tiff is, you might wanna take this."

Putting the call on speakerphone, I said: "I've got Alan on the line."

"Five grand for the guy who sliced up you and Gordy," Pen replied.

Piper's eyes widened. "They got Gordy, too?"

"You were lucky in comparison."

Alan stared at the scar above his waistband. "I'm not feeling lucky."

"You're still breathing, aren't you? I'd call that pretty fuckin' fortunate."

A glimmer of sadness seemed to change Piper's expression for a moment. "I'll give you three for their names."

"Five gets you one of 'em on a silver platter."

"And the other one?"

"He's gone, but I'm sure you'll get the location outta the lad who's kipping on my gurney."

"I'll send Eric with half now and you get the other half when I get the other half of the duo. Fair dos? Hello? Can you hear me, Pen?"

Pen had fallen into a silence that was punctuated only by heavy breathing. When he started talking again, it was in short, panicked bursts. "Oh, fuck me… Man, it's not whatcha think… Put it down, gadge… You don't wanna do… Put the fuckin' blade…."

The line went dead.

Piper told me to grab a gun from the drawer of his upstairs office, get my brother, and go to Pen's place in Guisborough. He gave me permission to take the keys to one of his sporty Jags and get over there 'Toot-fucking-sweet'.

I phoned my brother and told him about the change of plan. Then I pressed my foot down on the accelerator and raced off the estate.

2.

BILLY CHIN watched a trio of his favourite junkies fuck on a dirty mattress in the corner of the mould dappled living room he used as his base of operations. He told them to move faster, and clapped his hands repeatedly until the junkies matched his rhythm. As soon as they were all going at the right speed, Billy unzipped his fly and started masturbating. Then he told the girl to look at him. She responded by fixing him with her baby blues.

Yeah, that did the trick.

Despite all the shit she put in her veins, the girl was still pretty. Her tight frame hadn't yet succumbed to all her terrible life choices. It helped that she was only too happy to put on live performances for a fistful of skag. She grinned when her boss told her how hard his dick was.

The two men she was sandwiched between could always be relied upon to perform no matter how many substances they abused. Their desire to get high overcame any other issues they might have. They also grinned when he told them that they were getting the good shit tonight.

Billy took his pleasures where he could get them. Having AIDS meant he didn't partake in the sex, but he did at least get to enjoy watching the younger, prettier junkies having fun. The hotter the action, the better he paid. These three were certainly earning their shots tonight. If they finished as well as they had started he might even let them take one of the executive suites, which, in Billy's parlance, meant a room with a mattress and pillows rather than sleeping bags or blankets.

As the thrusting became more frenetic and frenzied, Billy matched them for speed, and urged them to go faster. As he felt himself moving towards an orgasm, his phone rang. He tried ignoring it but it didn't stop. The tone made his dick shrink and messed with the threesome's rhythm.

When he realised that the ringing wasn't going to end, Billy yanked the phone out of his back pocket, looked at the display, and screamed: "What? What the fuck d'you want, Pen?"

"I'm sorry I caught you at a bad time, mate. I thought you'd wanna know summat important."

"More important than watching three beautiful people fuck?"

"I... I think so?"

"You don't sound so sure."

The trio had slowed to the occasional thrust as they watched their boss with expectant gazes. He told them to keep going, so they got back into their rhythm. The girl started moaning again.

"Are there actual people fucking in your gaff, Bee?"

"I'm watching summat that those in the porn industry would term as a DP. Real and live and hot as shit, so you'd better have a really fuckin' good reason for this call. Otherwise, I'm gonna take your little finger as punishment."

"You don't need to threaten me, mate. I'm...."

"You sound like you're gonna cry, Pen. Are you gonna cry?"

"No... I'm...."

"Then dry your eyes and get to the point."

"I just got a call from Raffles."

"That's nice," Billy replied, not giving it much thought. "What's that useless spunk bubble up to these days?"

"Booking some medical treatment."

This pricked the dealer's interest. The hairs on his forearms rose to attention. He had the distinct feeling that he was about to be fucked as hard the junkies on the mattress.

"He said to put it on your tab."

Suddenly, the sex show seemed a lot less exciting. Billy's cock shrivelled until it disappeared within the wild thatch of his pubic hair. He sat upright and pressed the phone to his ear. Rage clouded all his other thoughts and one overriding idea settled in his mind: dragging a sharp serrated blade slowly across Raffles' scrawny throat.

"That cheeky bastard."

"Whatcha want me to do?"

"Keep him there."

The threesome had ended. The junkies watched him for further instructions. Billy clicked his fingers and hitched a thumb over his shoulder. "You three — fuck off upstairs."

"You mean you want me to treat him?" Pen asked.

"Put that piece of shit to sleep," Billy said, "and keep him that way until I get to your place."

"Okay. But what about a reward?"

Billy snorted laughter. "A reward? For what?"

"For telling you."

He had no intention of giving Pen a damn thing, but he wasn't going to let him know that. Instead, he said sure let's discuss it when I get there and hung up.

Billy went to a nearby squat that was also under his control and picked up a couple of heavies. They were big men who'd fallen on hard times. One had been a local bouncer back in the days before he discovered the fluffy cloud highs of heroin. The other was a bare knuckle boxer who'd refused to throw a fight and found legitimate work hard to come by in the aftermath. They were thankful for the employment.

Billy nodded and said: "You can thank me by keeping the fuckery to a minimum."

Despite the height and weight disparity between Billy and the two heavies, they took his words as they were intended: both as a demand for competence and a threat from the kind of man who was happy to ruthlessly dispose of anybody who displeased him. The man had lived to forty-three years of age, despite AIDS and Hepatitis and the kind of drug addiction that would kill lesser men, controlling an army of junkies and a network of drug squats, while dictating the flow of the local drug trade. His slight five-six frame wasn't much to look at, but if you made the mistake of crossing paths with Billy Chin, and somehow lived to tell the tale, you'd certainly remember the experience. He was a player.

"I'd take weapons, lads," he announced. "If Raff wakes up suddenly, he'll happily carve youse up like you're the Sunday roast."

3.

JAMES PENNINGTON found it hard to take his eyes off the blood-stained knife in Mary's hand, but when he noticed the desperation on the man's face, he ended the call and lowered the phone.

"It's not whatcha think."

"Are you a mind reader?"

"What?"

"It's a simple question."

"No, I'm not a mind reader."

"Then you have no idea what I'm thinking, do you?"

"Mebbe not, but I can guess."

"You're gonna serve up Raff on a 'silver platter' is what I'm thinking. At least, that's what I heard."

"Coz that's how I like to serve up toast. And sweetheart, Raffles is fuckin' toast."

As the colour drained from Mary's face, and he loosened his grip on the knife handle, Pen knew that he had nothing to fear. This man wasn't a killer. In fact, he barely even qualified as human. With his disfigured face and crushed spirit, he seemed more like a wraith that was forever doomed to walk among the living than an actual person.

Emboldened, Pen scooped up a scalpel and held it in front of him. The dismay that registered on Mary's face gave him further courage. "I've offered him up on a first come, first served basis. Either Billy Chin collects, or Alan Piper's gonna have him. Whichever way it goes, your friend's done, and I'm getting paid."

"How about I take him," Mary replied in a barely audible croak. "You gonna stop me?"

Pen smiled. "If I have to."

Mary went to say something but the surgeon cut him off. "Keep

Gordy's cash," he said. "Get the fuck outta here and start over, but you're not touching this prick."

The deepening distress on Mary's face convinced Pen that his opponent was about to turn and run away. It was the last mistake the surgeon ever made. What Pen mistook for fear and cowardice was in fact the grudging acceptance that if he wanted to save his friend, Mary would have to get his hands dirty. Pen lowered the scalpel but kept it pressed against his upper thigh. When he was at his most vulnerable, Mary rushed in and slammed the blade into the surgeon's chest and buried it to the hilt. Pen responded with several quick jabs into his attacker's stomach and left side before dropping to the floor with an open-mouthed expression of shock on his face.

"You silly prick," were his last words before his face slackened and his eyes lost their focus.

Despite the fact that Pen gave him little choice, Mary still felt revulsion and guilt that twisted his innards like they were party balloons. But the pain in his gut wasn't just down to remorse; his stomach and side were leaking blood. The bleeding wasn't quite a torrent, but it wasn't a trickle either.

Despite the fact that he knew he was making his injuries worse, Mary heaved his friend off the gurney, staggered down the stairs, and loaded him into the backseat of the car. He got in the driver's seat and drove out onto the moors until he could no longer see straight. He pulled off the road into a small tree lined grove and parked behind a tangle of tall shrubs.

With some difficulty because of the blood loss, Mary wrote down his account number, sort code, and a couple of pin numbers on an envelope that he found in the glove box, along with a note that said:

If you're reading this, I'm dead. Pen was gonna sell you to either Billy or Alan (whoever got there first). I saved you. I think you're worth saving. I've got forty grand in total. Twenty in my account, and twenty on the two currency cards in my pocket (first pin is the blue card, second is the red). Take it all. Do what you want with it. Get clean, get high. Choice is yours. But I really hope you get clean.

If you can, give me a decent burial. Otherwise, so long. You were probably my only friend. At least the only one who stuck by me when it mattered.

Your mate, Shawn

He put the bag of money on the seat beside him, then he closed his eyes and waited for the big sleep. It didn't take long to arrive.

Shawn Wilcox felt at peace when the moment came, and died believing that he was finally a hero.

4.

I OPENED the door gently and eased into the cramped entrance hall with my brother breathing down my neck. There were voices upstairs. One was instantly recognisable, but the others were a mystery. The recognisable voice was the loudest.

"We need to clean up this shite, and fast. Otherwise, we're gonna be getting our backdoors smashed in at Durham jail. Now I dunno about you two, but I've been there, done that, and got the virus to show for it. I don't wanna fuckin' repeat performance, thank you very much; so by the time we're finished, I want this place as clean and spotless as a virgin's box."

"So who's doing what?"

"Find the biggest suitcase you can find and fold him into it," Billy said. "Fuckin' break summat if you hafta. Seb, you need to clean the blood and surfaces. Then bleach the shit outta everything. I'm gonna pack clothes and documents. Mebbe find some cash if he's got any. Might as well get summat outta this clusterfuck."

I took out my mobile phone and got the camera ready. The phone was one of the few benefits of working for Piper, although it meant we were always at his beck and call. Still, it was useful when you wanted to do a little blackmail.

We crept upstairs and reached the landing as the door to Pen's home-made surgery creaked open. That provided a beautifully framed shot of Billy Chin and a large skinhead associate standing over the bloody corpse of James Pennington. The heavy-set thug who opened the door stared at us with an idiotic expression of surprise on his face.

He groaned and said: "BC, we've got guests."

Billy glowered in our direction. "Whadda you homos want?"

"We came for some medical advice."

Billy noticed the camera in my hand and grinned. "Well, here's summat for free: Doctor Chin advises youse to drop the camera phone and fuck off back the way you came, otherwise you're gonna have a *genuine* medical emergency."

"No can do."

Billy shrugged and clicked his fingers. "Teach these idiots a lesson. Fuck em up, Josh. Gerrus the phone."

The big man stormed forward and made an unsubtle grab for the handset that my brother blocked with a shoulder barge. Josh flashed a lightning right, that my brother sidestepped, and followed with a gutshot that was deflected with an elbow. The man responded with a flurry of fists that he threw in my brother's direction that were either dodged or diverted with some well timed blocks.

My brother slammed his forehead into his opponent's face, flattening his nose, buried a low right into the bulge of his gut, sending the remains of his McDonald's Happy Meal splashing across the floorboards, and flipped him over his shoulder and down the stairs, where he landed with a crunch. He didn't get up again.

My brother admired his handiwork for a moment before turning towards Billy and his other associate. "You wanna dance, Sinead?"

The skinhead backed away with his hands raised. "I came here for support, boss. Not whatever the fuck this is."

Billy looked aghast. "Are you having a laugh, mate? Gerrin there, Seb, you fuckin' fanny."

Seb shook his head again. "This shit's above me pay grade."

"Pay grade? Whaddaya think this is, a fuckin' union meeting? Get the fuck in there, you retard, mash him up."

Seb started walking away. "No, thanks. I've seen him in action on the doors, boss. This prick's hospitalised more bouncers than cancer. You're on your own."

The skinhead moved close to my brother with his hands raised. "Lemme past, please."

My brother shuffled to one side. "Try owt funny and your next laugh'll be through a broken jaw."

"I don't much feel like laughing tonight," he replied, rushing down the stairs. He stepped over his injured associate and stumbled out of the door.

We turned towards Billy, who was holding a syringe full of blood

— his own — ready to inject whoever was stupid enough to get close to him with a fresh dose of HIV and Hep. "Fuckin' oway then, lads, if you fancy summa me."

My brother hesitated. We'd had run-ins with him in the past, back when he was foolish enough to borrow money from our boss at extortionate rates of interest, and his favourite trick was faking illness, then springing a surprise needle to the throat. Billy had caught out my brother with this ruse a couple of years ago. It's the only time I've seen him genuinely terrified.

"I'm not going near him," he insisted.

This made Billy grin.

I pulled the gun I'd borrowed from Piper.

He stopped grinning.

"You're gonna hafta kill me, dickhead."

"That can be arranged," I replied and lined up my shot. "Or we can talk."

"What've *we* gotta talk about?"

My mind went back to the cash underneath Henry Mansell's floorboards. We couldn't take *that* money but there was nothing stopping us from taking it from other dealers. All we needed was the right information and a bit of luck. I'd been considering a new line of business for a while. In the long run, working for Piper was a dead end. If I wanted to make bank, I'd have to go into business for myself. And what better way to make money than to steal it from the kinds of people who couldn't go to the police.

"Information."

"Such as?"

"The comings and goings of local dealers. Preferably idiots with poor security."

Billy grinned. "What's in it for me?"

"Firstly, these pictures stay on this camera."

"Please continue, coz that's currently what I call a 'fuck you deal'. As in, fuck you if you think I'm having any part of *that*. Just gimme a bullet instead."

"*Secondly*, if you let me finish, you'll get ten percent of the profits, plus whatever junky you send our way gets a flat fee in exchange for what they know," I replied. "And after six jobs, I'll delete the pics."

Billy shook his head, believing there was a negotiation to be had, and said: "Equal split, and a flat fee of five hundred for the junkies."

"Here's *our* final offer: twenty to you, and as for your junkies we'll give 'em two-fifty before the job and the same again after. That's the best deal you're gonna get."

Billy thought about this, put away his syringe, and extended a hand. "Okay, you've gotta deal, so long as you help me clean up *this* shite."

I hesitated a moment, because Billy wasn't exactly trustworthy, and handed the gun to my brother. "If he stabs me, shoot him."

Derek snatched the weapon as the junky's laughter reverberated around the house.

"Six jobs, right?" he said, coming towards me.

"That's right."

"After which, you'll delete those pictures?"

"Yeah."

"Then shake on it, you cunt."

We shook hands and maintained eye contact until Billy pulled back his hand and stepped away. "Now let's clean this shit."

"I'll do you one better," I replied. "You tell me who did this and I'll get Piper to tidy the mess."

Not being one to turn down the chance of an easy getaway, Billy offered an immediate response: "Raffles."

"Which means the second guy's probably Mary."

Billy gave me a sardonic thumbs up, meaning he no longer gave a shit now that someone else was dealing with things.

"Yeah, cool story, bruv," Billy said as he descended the stairs. He stopped to wake up his unconscious associate. The big man looked up in a daze and asked what happened.

"I found out that you're as useful as a chocolate dildo," Billy hissed. "Rise and shine, fucktard. Nap time's over."

The big man wobbled unsteadily to his feet and followed his boss through the front door and out into the street.

My brother turned to me. "Is this evening over yet?"

"Not quite," I replied as I held the phone to my ear. "Hey, how're you doing? I'd like to order some Mr Muscle, please."

5.

WHEN RAFFLES woke, he blinked in confusion at the milky daylight, groaned in pain, and glanced around nervously. The change of surroundings suggested to him that something had gone badly wrong. Noticing Mary asleep in the front seat, Raffles prodded his shoulder. "Mate, what the hell happened back there?"

When his friend didn't respond, Raffles shook him by the shoulder and said: "Ow, sleepyhead, rise and…."

Mary slumped forward against the steering wheel. Raffles looked down at the blood-soaked carpet and driver's seat. He cursed, stumbled out of the car, and went around to the front of the vehicle. Raffles pulled his friend back and stared at him; his pallid, gaunt face seemed to have a trace of a smile. Raffles caressed the cold flesh of his face with his fingers and hoped that the smile meant he went peacefully.

The bag of money caught his eye, so he went around to the other side of the car and swiped it along with the scrap of paper. There was something heartfelt about the note that made him choke up. He wiped his eyes and whispered: "You deserved better."

Raffles' broken hand ensured he couldn't dig a grave for his friend, but he sure as hell could give him a decent burial. First, he smashed Mary's face with a rock and removed his teeth, to slow down any attempts at identification, and give him the opportunity to distance himself from the mess. He knew DNA could speed up the process, but even that would take the police a while. He stopped a couple of times and stepped away from the vehicle to catch his breath and gather his thoughts. Doing this to his friend turned his stomach, but it was the only thing he could think of to distance himself from the mess. Once finished, he sat on a fallen tree trunk and sobbed.

Then Raffles wiped his eyes, readied himself, and gave Mary his best interpretation of a Viking funeral. He broke one of his disposable lighters in half and poured the fluid over some carefully positioned rags on the front and back seats, and used an entire box of matches to start a fire. He hung around and watched the flames until they raged throughout the interior, sending thick black smoke skyward, then he turned and walked away. Raffles cut through fields of purple heather and past thickets of spindly trees and shrubs, following the road at a distance, until the pain of his throbbing hand became too much to bear. Raffles phoned an acquaintance to come and collect him from beside a rocky promontory not far from a narrow gravel track road.

The taxi ride cost him five hundred quid of Gordy's money, along with another grand for a visit to a vet in Danby. The doctor gave him a shot of heroin and proceeded to straighten his crooked fingers. He wasn't blessed with a gentle bedside manner, and the drugs only just managed to take the edge off the pain. As soon as his digits were in splints, the vet helped him into a sling, and told him he could spend two nights in the spare room for another five hundred. Raffles paid the fee and tried recuperating on a lumpy single bed surrounded by box files with only some paracetamol for the pain.

He used the time to dissect in explicit detail how he'd used his friend's plight to fulfil a personal vendetta against Gordy and Piper. An enormous weight of guilt settled over him. His immediate response was to buy twenty grand of heroin and self-medicate his way through the remorse. He let the feeling pass and decided on something that Mary would approve of: cleaning up his act and getting out of Teesside. He knew it would be difficult and painful, but he figured he deserved his share of pain for what he'd done.

When his two days were up, with withdrawal symptoms wracking his body, Raffles took a trip by train to Leeds. He spent the journey shivering and trying not to shit himself. Every judder in the carriage sent pain through his muscles and into his bones. Every gut spasm folded him over and sent him into a panic that he was going to flood the compartment with diarrhoea. He kept his head down and ignored the passengers who muttered insults as they passed by.

The moment he arrived at the station, Raffles stumbled off the train, bumping shoulders with hordes of commuters in his haste to get by, rushed into a dirty cubicle, and spent the next half an hour spraying the toilet bowl with withdrawal shits. At one point the pain was so intense, he worried that he was about to have a rectal prolapse. When he was sure there was nothing else inside him, he gathered enough strength to make it out of the station and onto a bus to Chapeltown.

He staggered off the bus and hobbled to his brother's pebbledash terrace and knocked on the door. It opened and a tall bald man with flushed cheeks looked at the sweat soaked shadow in his doorway, sighed, and folded his arms.

"Are you tryna get clean? Or are you just wasting my time?"

Raffles tried to speak but couldn't. His jaw and tongue moved without generating any sounds. Marlon Mulherne shook his big head and started to close the door with his foot.

"I'm getting too old for this shit, Daz. We both are. Do you wanna get clean or not?"

It took all of Raffles' strength just to nod.

His brother blocked the entrance. "I wanna hear you say it. *Then* I'll believe it."

"I want... to get clean."

"Will you go to meetings?"

"Y...Yes."

"And when you're well again, will you apologise to Dad for what you did to him?"

"Marlon...."

"I'm serious, lad. It's all or nothing. And if it's nothing, then get the hell off my step and go someplace else, coz I'm sick of half measures."

"I'll apologise."

His brother stepped aside.

"Come on in," he said. "Don't even think about talking to the missus or the kids."

"Yeah, I know, you'll kick me out."

Marlon smiled. "No mate, I'll fucking kill you."

PART FOUR: SHIT HAPPENS

1.

NEARLY SIX months clean and Raffles was feeling the pull. But it wasn't the habit tugging at his sleeves, it was the knowledge that the man responsible for Mary hadn't paid the price. Gordy might have snapped his leg on Piper's orders, but it was Jezza who'd put him in frame. The prick had sold out one of his best friends for a few doses of smack. Raffles had done some terrible shit over the years, but he drew the line at betraying his mates.

He sat in meetings and listened to other addicts talk about forgiveness and coming to terms with the past without ever really hearing their words. He nodded his head at the right times and made all the right noises, but he was unable to grasp the concept of letting go of his rage. Whenever Raffles spoke eloquently about his addiction, and lied convincingly about harbouring no grudges, images of Jeremy Collins' gaunt face flashed through his head. He imagined killing the prick in numerous gratifying ways, and every time his brain rewarded him with a small shot of serotonin.

Raffles soon realised that revenge had replaced heroin as his drug of choice, and the only fix he gave a damn about was the poisoned one he intended to give Jeremy Collins for his part in Mary's death. He believed he owed his friend that much, at least, and began making plans on how he was going to get back to Boro and buy drugs without drawing attention. Getting clean, and putting on the weight he'd lost over the years, was a big part of his scheme. As soon as his hand healed, Raffles hit the gym and packed on the muscle, working his body to the limit even when he was fed up and bored. He cut out the junk food and the booze and transformed himself. Whenever Raffles looked at his old photos and compared them with where he was now the transformation was like night and day.

He didn't tell his brother about the plan, mostly because he would have tried to talk him out of it, but also because he didn't want Marlon to think he'd failed in some way. Raffles had been angry his whole life. None of that rage was his brother's fault.

He travelled to Boro on the earliest available train because no junkies or villains would be awake at this time. Most of them were creatures of the night, or at the very least the late afternoon. Most of them thought dawn was the name of some girl they once fucked.

He got off the train and vacated the station quickly, keeping his head high as he played the role of Darren Mulherne to a tee. His skin had colour, aided with a little fake tan, the dark crescents beneath his eyes had disappeared, his chestnut hair was neatly trimmed, and he'd taken the time to iron his white shirt and black chinos and put a shine on his brogues. Then he put on an expensive new jacket he'd bought the day before. His working man disguise was solid, and he was positive most of his associates wouldn't recognise him, but even so, he didn't want to hang around long enough for junky memories to flicker into life and put a name to a familiar face.

He decided to avoid the usual haunts of St Hilda's and Middlesbrough and instead took a cab to South Bank and a dealer he only used when things were really desperate. Yannis Kyriakos — also known as Yannis K, Yannis The K, Special K, Y2K, and Yan The Man — dealt with so many wretched souls that he wouldn't remember Raffles now that he was clean and sober.

Yannis' place was a derelict terrace with secure metal fixings on the door and windows at the front, which was why all the serious business happened at the back. Pallid junkies waited on various parts of a shit strewn patch of grass for someone to lead them to the promised land. They tried to look casual, like they belonged, which was a joke. Now that he was sober, Raffles realised that nothing stood out more than junkies trying to act naturally. When it was his turn, the rat-faced dogsbody that Yannis sent out to fetch him, took one look at his clothes, shook his head, and hitched a thumb over his scrawny shoulder.

"Get fucked, narc."

Back when things were desperate, Raffles had shared a needle with this idiot. Somehow, through blind luck, he'd managed to avoid the various illnesses that ruined most junkies, particularly the ones who shared gear. Despite this, Del Ennis didn't recognise his old shooting partner. In fact, he came in close and said: "Didn't you hear me, Clean Shirt?"

Raffles fluttered two twenties in front of the man's face. "I heard you fine, but I wanna get fed. And I want you to help me."

Del snatched the notes out of his hand, put them in his pocket, and said: "Follow me."

They walked past a gaggle of smackheads who grumbled about queue jumpers, through a high-walled backyard that was also lined with impatient addicts, and into a room that had once been a kitchen but was now just an empty shell with ancient wall tiles and huge murals of black mould. A junky napped in the corner with a needle in his arm and his paraphernalia scattered around him on the dirty lino.

They went through into a small candle lit living room that reeked of vinegar and sweat. Yannis' burly frame was wedged between the arms of a ragged armchair. He was bald and barrel-chested with a heavy cheeked face that could have been anywhere from a rough thirty to a smooth sixty. There was a small sofa on the other side of the room with a thin naked woman asleep on it. The dealer eyed his visitors with curiosity, then he waved his hand at Del, who took that as his cue to leave. Yannis remained in his chair and looked Raffles up and down repeatedly. He was worried that the dealer had recognised him right up until the moment he hissed: "Ow, working man, I think you're in the wrong fuckin' place."

Once upon a time, when cash was tight, and his desperation for a fix was at its worst, Yannis had made him suck his cock in exchange for a watery fix of methadone that was barely worth the effort to inject. Raffles remembered the dealer slapping his face and calling him *bitch* as he worked his magic on the man's small semi-erect dick, rolling it around his mouth like the world's worst soft-boiled sweet.

The memory made him want to gag, but he maintained his calm. He wondered why the dealer couldn't remember his face, especially when he'd spent a good ten minutes fucking it back in the day. Raffles contemplated how many people Yannis had abused over the years, then cast the thought aside because it made him angry. Instead, he replied: "Gimme some Mexican brown, and a couple of grains of Tango."

The dealer's thick eyebrows went up in question marks of surprise, then his small grey eyes narrowed. He ran a hand along his shaved head and flashed his bejewelled grills.

"Well, whoop-de-fuckin'-do, Clean Shirt knows his shit. Course, you coulda learnt all that at bacon school, with all the other little piglets."

"I'm not a policeman."

Yannis revealed his grills again and whispered: "So make like a faggot and lift that fuckin' shirt. I wanna see bare flesh, working man, otherwise you're out on the pavement. I've got no fuckin' time for arguments. You wanna feed? Show me you're not wired up like a bitch."

"I told you before, I'm not bacon."

"Methinks the piggy doth protest too much."

Tired of arguing, Raffles raised the shirt to his chest and did a little pirouette. This pleased the dealer.

"Okay, gadge, it's sixty for the Brown and another sixty for the Dance Fever."

"A bit steep."

"The price is the price, and if you don't like it, you can make like a tree and go fuck yourself."

"I don't think that's how the saying goes."

"That so?" he said. "Now, what kinda self-respecting working man doesn't know that many trees self-pollinate?"

"The kind that comes to South Bank for his brown."

"You shoulda spent more time in school," he replied. "Now pay up and disappear, before I lose my cheery disposition."

As Raffles stuffed the cash into the dealer's big hand, Yannis leaned in and said: "Do I know you from somewhere, gadge?"

A momentary spike of adrenaline sent his heart-rate through the roof. Raffles was certain he bore almost no resemblance to the wretched creature that last shuffled through these doors. Even so, his brain started formulating escape plans. If things got really bad, there was always the switchblade in his back pocket.

"Nah mate, I got a recommendation from a friend."

"Oh yeah, who?"

Raffles searched his memory for a few junkies he hung with back when he was getting methadone scraps from Yannis. "Steve-O."

"Jones or Williams?"

He was fishing for info, but it was hard to work out if this was because Yannis still didn't believe he was a working man, or if he was beginning to remember their intimate encounter.

"Fucked if I know," Raffles said. "We're not *that* close; just work together sometimes. He looks like Jarvis Cocker with AIDS."

"Oh yeah, I know him," he said. "Came here last week with that Goth slut. Whatshername?"

Raffles shrugged. "Never seen him with a woman. I always thought he was a puff."

"Surprised at that," he replied. "They're pretty tight. Although not so tight that he didn't make her gimme a blowie when he was low on funds the other week."

Yannis laughed at the memory. "The silly prick sat on that sofa, with a face like a wet weekend in Whitby, as Whatshername gave me the Linda Lovelace treatment. At one point, I thought he was gonna cry when I started smacking her in the face and calling her bitch…"

The dealer paused for a moment, and Raffles saw the recognition in his eyes. This was quickly replaced by a superficial smile. "Lemme go get your shit now."

A smirk and a knowing crack at Raffles' expense would have been enough for him to know that everything was fine, but the change in mood set him on edge. Yannis moved towards the sofa. He kept his gear in its hollowed out base, but it was also where he kept a revolver.

Deciding it was better to be safe than sorry, Raffles put a hand in his back pocket and brushed his fingers along the switchblade handle. Quietly, he closed the distance between them while the dealer's back was turned.

While he was sobering up, Raffles had made a few enquiries in the aftermath of what happened with him and Mary. What he found out didn't surprise him. Piper had a five grand contract on his life, and even Billy Chin was offering a grand for his whereabouts.

Yannis budged the sleeping woman out of the way, lifted the far left cushion, and rummaged inside. Raffles eased the switchblade from his back pocket and brought it to his side with his finger on the button. He moved within a couple of steps of the dealer and waited.

Raffles remembered that the drugs were in a metal container with loose coins rattling around inside. He didn't hear anything as distinctive as that, but what he did catch was the click of a revolver hammer being drawn back. As the dealer turned, Raffles pressed the switch and started swinging. The gun boomed. Something hit Raffles' gut with the force of a fist, but he ignored the pain and plunged his blade into the dealer's neck. Working quickly, he hacked through thick cords of muscle and cut the hard tube of his attacker's windpipe. Blood gushed. Yannis gargled. He dropped the gun, then collapsed. His hands went to his neck in a futile attempt to stop himself from bleeding to death. There was a brief flicker of fear in the man's eyes that was gone by the time Raffles had scooped the revolver off the ground.

There was a thump of heavy feet on the stairs, which probably belonged to one of Yannis' bodyguards. Raffles rolled the dead dealer on his side, got on the ground, and used his corpse as a shield. A well-built baldy came through the hallway door, wearing only a pair of black socks, firing a semi-automatic wildly and missing everything but the walls. Raffles stayed calm and put a round into the man's cock and balls. Baldy shrieked, dropped his weapon, and hit the floor with a crash. He surveyed the damage to his other weapon and started to whimper.

Raffles got off the ground, grabbed the semi-auto, and pressed the hot gun barrel to the man's temple and asked him what to say when the police came to the crime scene. Baldy just about managed to croak that they were attacked by an Asian man in his fifties, before cradling his ruined genitals and curling up on the dirty carpet.

Raffles went back to the sofa. Somehow, the naked woman was still in a deep sleep and had remained undisturbed by all the gunfire. He worked fast and withdrew four stacks of notes from inside the chair. As he was putting the money in various pockets, he noticed the bleeding wound on the left side of his stomach just below the ribcage. He checked to see if the bullet had exited at the back; there wasn't any blood, so he had at least managed to avoid that additional trauma. The pain wasn't too bad at the moment but, as his blood loss increased and shock began to take hold, Raffles knew this was temporary. So he needed to move while it was still possible.

Expecting more heavies, Raffles went into the kitchen with his revolver at the ready. Aside from the sleeping junky in the corner there was nobody around. The courtyard was also empty. The grassy area behind the houses was deserted; the junkies ran at the first sign of trouble.

Raffles looked at his wound. It wasn't bleeding as badly as he expected, but it still didn't look great. He carefully zipped up his jacket to cover the mess. The ruse might hold for a bit, helped by the dark blue jacket and black chinos, but it was a matter of urgency that he grabbed a car before he could no longer walk.

He moved as quickly as he could considering the pain and lurched into a side road in search of a car to commandeer. A vehicle pulled up beside him and revved its engine. Raffles thought about pulling the revolver, but the two men pointing weapons at him looked happy to put him down before he had a chance to draw.

"You can do this the easy way or the gory way," the man in the passenger seat said. "I really don't give a fuck."

As long as he managed to get the hot dose to Jezza, it didn't really matter what happened to him now.

"Let's do it easy," he replied.

2.

DEL ENNIS immediately recognised the prick in the working man outfit. Despite the gym muscles and the healthy complexion and the expensive haircut, it was obvious that this idiot was the junky formerly known as Raffles.

Del pretended not to know him and even told him to leave the queue, but Raffles was insistent and handed him forty quid to get an audience with his boss. Del kept up the pretence and walked him past a line of junkies who complained and hollered.

It amused him that Raffles thought his disguise was impeccable. Getting clean didn't change the shape of one's face or alter the colour of the eyes. Del had shared needles with this man, he'd watched him suck Yannis' cock for a shitty methadone fix. You don't forget stuff like that, even if you want to.

They went through the stripped out shell of a house that reeked of mould, vinegar and piss and into a candle lit living room. Yannis lounged in an armchair in his T-shirt and boxers, still sweating after his session with a naked woman who was curled up on the sofa.

The dealer eyed them with an expression that to the untrained eye looked like curiosity but was in fact disgust. Yannis hadn't yet recognised his well dressed visitor, but Del didn't want to be around when the penny finally dropped, so he took the opportunity to leave quickly when his boss told him to vanish.

As soon as he was outside, Del moved out of earshot of the loose collection of junkies waiting near the house, took out his phone and made a call. Alan Piper had put five grand on Raffles' head, and his people were actively looking to collect it. Assuming the guy got out of Yannis' place alive, Del intended to make sure he got some kind of finder's fee.

The Stanton brothers had been hanging around Yannis' place recently, presumably on the lookout for Raffles, which had Del wondering what they might be prepared to offer as payment. Del got Eric's number from a friend and made a few calls. There was finally an answer on the third attempt.

"I don't recognise this number, fucko, so you better have a good reason for calling me."

"Are you lads still looking for Raffles?"

"Yeah, sure."

"And if I give you information that'll put him in your laps — what'd summat like that be worth to you?"

"Ten percent."

Five hundred quid was decent money, but he wondered if there was room for negotiation. "Let's make it a grand."

"I can make it nowt, if you want, by telling you to go fuck yourself, and getting on with the rest of my day."

"Then why the fuck have you been camped out at Yannis' joint over the last week?"

There was a pause. "Who the fuck is this?"

"Del."

"Ennis?"

There was another pause. "Piper had solid info that Raffles might show his fizz around there."

It was a lie. Del wasn't sure how he knew, but there was something about Eric's tone that wasn't right. He decided not to push the topic any further because he wanted the money. Besides, it wasn't any of his business. Instead, he decided to use Piper as a negotiation tactic.

"Then your boss might not be too happy to find out you had summat to give him, and decided instead to do nowt."

"Whyn't we split the difference and make it seven-fifty? If you ask for a grand again, I'm gonna hang up on you."

It was better than nothing, so Del said sure, it was a deal. Just as he was about to tell them to hurry a couple of shots rang out.

"Oh, fuck me. Somebody's turned the place into a fuckin' shooting range."

Junkies rushed in all directions. One of Yannis' two heavies, the one who always bragged about his gangster exploits, peered into the courtyard as another couple of gunshots echoed around the estate, then he turned around and walked away calmly without looking back.

Del put the phone to his ear, but the call had ended. The area was deserted; the junkies were gone, a few nosy neighbours peered through curtain gaps and dirty glass, but nobody was brave enough to call the police.

There weren't any sirens yet. In another five minutes, when the neighbours were feeling courageous enough to pick up their phones, there would be. It was time to get the fuck out of here. Del suspected he needed to find a new employer, because he was certain that his current one was dead.

3.

MARY'S DEATH made the news briefly. An unidentified male was found burnt to a crisp inside the vehicle of a local loan shark who was conveniently missing. The police put two and two together, worked out that it was five, and went looking for their main suspect: Gordon 'Gordy' Willis.

Of course, they wouldn't find him. He'd been shaved, defanged, chopped up, and fed to some pigs. He was gone forever. What was left of him was probably fertilising some farmer's soil. Like the police case, he was now just a load of shit.

After saving his life, and replacing Gordy as his favourite, Alan Piper had newfound respect for us. He gave us cushy jobs on better pay, and even let us have time off on bank holidays.

None of that stopped us from fixing our sights on something bigger. Billy Chin had been true to his word and sent us to some of the most shambolic operations I've laid eyes on. Dealers and thugs who were high on their own supply, thieves with fat stacks of cash stuffed under the mattress, an amateur loan shark with a safe code that went sequentially from one to six. Shambolic, or as Billy put it: "Fuckin' shambollocks, mate."

Yannis Kyriakos was the trickiest of the six. Like a couple of the names he'd given us, the dealer was one of Billy's direct competitors. According to the source, Yannis dealt watered down product at inflated prices, and liked to fuck anybody who couldn't afford the fee. Apparently, he did a lot of fucking. Men, women, pensioners, teenagers, Y2K didn't care who he screwed. Gender and age meant nothing to him, his kink was power, and what got him hard was the knowledge that his victims hated every second of it.

According to Billy, and he'd been right about everything else up to now, Yannis had two stashes. The one he could afford to lose that he kept within a hollowed out sofa, along with his product, and the one he *couldn't* afford to lose that lay behind a fake wall grate in his bedroom.

So when Del Ennis phoned with news about Raffles, I assumed that my number was the first one he could find. What I hadn't anticipated was that he'd seen us scoping the place out. It was immediately obvious that I'd been too casual and taken the stupidity of others for granted. Maybe because the other five jobs had been so easy, I'd assumed that hitting Yannis would be a doddle.

Del's call was a good thing; it meant he didn't suspect we were planning to raid his boss. I made an error by feeding him a line of bullshit about Piper, but it didn't sound convincing. Del knew it was a lie because he turned it into a negotiating tactic. I allowed him to talk me up from my starting offer, but as soon as I threatened to walk away from the deal, Del decided that a little bit of something was better than a whole lot of nothing.

The gunfire started just as we reached an agreement. We were about five minutes from Y2K's place, driving to a greasy spoon that my brother insisted did the best fry-up in Teesside, so I told him to turn the car around and get there in four.

He did it in three and a half.

A lot of speed limits were broken. Some pavements were mounted.

I'd written off Yannis' money, but there was still the possibility that Raffles had made it out alive. The five grand bounty on his head was better than nothing.

We saw him staggering up King Street. He was wearing a dark jacket that he'd zipped to the collar. Nothing suspicious about that on a balmy Spring day.

Raffles stopped by a car door and started fiddling with it in the hope that it was unlocked. We pulled up alongside him and revved the engine. Then we pulled our guns.

Raffles took a long pause. It was possible that he was considering pulling one of the weapons he'd taken from Yannis. I helped him with his decision by announcing:

"You can do this the easy way or the gory way. I really don't give a fuck."

He turned towards us slowly, his face pale, his breathing laboured and replied:

"Let's do it easy."

Raffles didn't have long to live, so he didn't waste time with excuses or regrets.

"I took a bunch of money and drugs outta Yannis' place. It's yours to keep, along with whatever your boss gives youse for my corpse. But I want summat in return."

"What's to stop us from taking all that shit off you when you pass?"

"Nowt, I s'pose. But in my pocket there's also a currency card with two gees on it. Only I know the pin."

"You could be bullshitting us," I said without actually believing it.

"And you could just take my pin, then fuck me over. It's not like I can do owt about it. I'm gonna hafta go on trust."

He had a point. We were going to come out of this a hell of a lot better than Raffles. The best he could hope for was that he died before Piper got his hands on him. It wasn't much of a deal.

"Okay, let's say I believe you."

"Lemme stop you there, gadge. I couldn't give a fuck if you believe me or not. I'm probably gonna pass out in a few minutes. Then I'm gonna die. We either make this deal *now*, or you can watch me croak in slow motion. I couldn't care less. In fact, I ceased to give a fuck about my future the second I got in the back of this shit pile you're driving."

Impending death was making Raffles disarmingly honest. It made me wonder where he'd been the last six months, but I also knew he had neither the time nor the strength to tell me. Instead I asked him what he wanted.

"In my pocket is a hot dose… deliver it to Jezza… you know Jezza?"

"Collins?"

He nodded. "Get it to him."

"Why?"

"He told Piper where to find Mary that day."

Which was true. Jezza called Piper, who promised him fifty if his info was solid, and then he contacted us. All this chaos for a pittance.

"That shit happened over a year ago," I said. "You should let it go."

"Would you?"

"Probably not."

Raffles head dropped momentarily, then jerked up, and a look of panic settled on his face. "Will you do it?"

"Sure."

I owed Del three-quarters for the tip. I was sure that an even grand would be enough money for him to personally deliver Jezza's hot dose.

The panic dissipated and was replaced by a dreamy expression that indicated he was readying himself for the afterlife. Raffles whispered his PIN a couple of times, closed his eyes and curled up on the back seat.

Piper toe-poked the comatose man on the ground several times and curled his lip disdainfully.

"You want five grand for *this?*"

"Dead or alive, you said."

"He's somewhere in between."

"Dead *or* alive," I replied.

Tall towers of broken vehicles creaked and groaned behind us. Gaz Feldman's scrapyard was like a forgotten city built out of ruined automobiles. Avenues of rusting steel opened out into the centre of the compound where the owner had his office, magnetic crane and crusher. Piper watched one of the stacks sway momentarily before turning back to the disappointment on the floor.

"I'm not paying for this shit."

Gaz Feldman smirked. It didn't do his toad-like face any favours. He didn't care. He was about to get several grand for body and vehicle disposal regardless of what Alan was saying right now.

"You *are* paying for this shit," he said. "Otherwise you're taking this fuckin' body with you on your way out. And we'll *never* do business again. This is what happens when you waste my time."

Piper's new right-hand man, a tall black guy named Toney T, decided this was the moment to make his presence felt. He stepped in close to the little scrapyard owner. "You wanna watch your mouth, gadge."

Believing he was doing Piper a favour, the tall man had actually just put his boss right in the shit. What Toney didn't realise was that this was how the loan shark conducted business. He complained for a while, tried his hand at negotiating, and then reluctantly paid the asking price. It was his way of maintaining his dignity in situations that were beyond his control. But now, thanks to Toney's stupidity, it wasn't his dignity he needed to worry about. They were both in genuine danger of losing their lives.

Feldman's place was hallowed turf, neutral ground. Gang rivalries stayed outside the gates. Bad attitudes weren't tolerated, and you sure as hell didn't raise your voice and threaten the owner on home territory, unless you were looking for a nasty case of shut-eye.

My brother gave me a sideways glance and we stepped away from the two men, putting as much space between us as possible. Piper cringed in fear and grabbed his sidekick's arm to stop things from getting worse.

He was too late.

Seemingly from out of nowhere, Gaz produced a small revolver that he jammed into Toney's abdomen, just above his belt buckle. A couple of men with shotguns emerged from opposite sides of the clearing and looked at their boss for further orders. We were one nod away from a bloodbath.

"I really hope your little helper didn't know that this place is Switzerland, Pretty Boy, coz if he's showing his shit on your orders, you're *both* going in the fuckin' soil."

Piper's shop bought tan lost several shades of lustre and his face tightened into an ugly grimace. He stepped close to Toney and whispered in his ear. The big man's bottom lip trembled as he realised how close he was to death. "Sorry, boss man," he replied. "I got over-excited and shit. Didn't mean nowt by it."

Feldman moved back a couple of steps but his finger stayed on the trigger. "I'll let it slide coz you're a newbie," he said, turning his cold gaze on Piper. "But *you* ought to know better about pulling that kinda shit in here."

"Look, I...."

"Shut the fuck up."

Piper hung his head. "I'm sorry, man. I should've explained the rules to him."

"Yeah, I know. And it's gonna cost you. Your rates have just doubled."

Piper shuffled uncomfortably.

"Oh, I'm sorry, mate, have you got summat you wanna add to this conversation? Would you like to make a complaint?"

The loan shark shook his head.

"I didn't think so," Gaz said. "Now you *will* pay for the body. Otherwise, every fucker in Teesside'll find out you don't honour your promises. Then they'll find out you had this prick pull a gun on neutral ground."

"But he didn't...."

"Yeah, but it'll be *my* word against yours. And by the time I've finished with you, your word won't mean shit around here. Or alternatively, we can just end it here and now."

The two men with shotguns raised their weapons. We put further distance between us and Piper.

The loan shark held out a shaking hand towards Toney and clicked his fingers. The big guy reached carefully into a holdall, removed a brown leather folio case, and rested it on the open palm. Piper unzipped it, pulled out five grand, and tossed it in my direction. I swiped the bundle out of the air and stuffed it in an inside pocket. I tried not to act like I was weighed down with cash.

"Whaddaya wanna do with him?" I asked.

Piper stamped on Raffles' head several times, then removed another couple of grand from the folio and handed it to Feldman.

"For the corpse and the car."

"I think you're forgetting summat."

Piper huffed. "I'll get you the other half later in the week."

"With interest. Your usual Vig."

The loan shark's jaw muscles flexed but he kept his opinion to himself. "Sure."

"Don't make me come looking for you."

Piper turned and fast-walked out of the clearing with Toney T trailing behind him.

Feldman patted me on the shoulder. "I don't think that new fella's gonna last."

"He'll be lucky if he's still employed at the end of the day."

Feldman pocketed the pistol and nodded to his underlings. They took the hint and disappeared back into the maze of wreckage. "You lads might wanna make yourselves scarce," he said. "This shit's gonna get bloody."

★★★

The split came to six grand each (with a grand put aside for Del). After a little whining from my brother, it became seven and five in his favour. He argued that the junky's money should also come out of my share, but I countered that it might be better if he went and fucked himself instead.

Del was somewhat surprised when I told him I had his money. His astonishment increased when I told him to meet me near the old Town Hall.

This seemed like the ideal place for it to come to an end.

A sharp wind cut in from the river and made waves in the long grey grass. A couple of dickheads with Hilda's Boys ink on their forearms gave me the evil eye as they did their rounds. They exchanged words as they walked away. I knew they would be back with reinforcements. In fact, I was counting on it.

Del emerged from the back garden of a nearby derelict and approached with a hesitant stride, like a dog that's not sure if it's getting a treat or a beating. When he was close enough, Del took in his surroundings with a couple of shifty glances, and whispered: "I really didn't expect you to come."

"Is that why you were hiding?"

He nodded. "The HBs don't fuck around. And if they think we're doing business on their turf, they'll gouge out our eyeballs and piss in the holes."

"Let me worry about them," I said as I handed him the cash. He counted it quickly, with junky dexterity, because he was used to making hasty deals. I held the other two-fifty in his eyeline. As he pocketed his reward, Del noticed what was in my hand and licked his lips nervously.

"What's that for?"

"Delivering a hot dose to Jezza."

"Jezza Collins?"

"That's right."

Del frowned. "Why?"

"Coz it was the last wish of a dying man."

"Raffles?"

I nodded.

"Not being funny or nowt, but since when've you given a shit about dying men?"

"Since one more or less croaked in the back seat of my brother's car trying to get revenge for his best friend."

"I just figured he was back on the powder."

"He came back here to finish a job he started over six months ago. He got Gordy and my boss."

"Piper lived."

"Yeah, but Alan frets at night about that scar across his abdomen. It really fuckin' bothers him. And considering how vain he is, he hates the fact that it's a blemish on his otherwise flawless beauty. He's visited at least two plastic surgeons about it. That counts as successful revenge in my book."

"And Jezza?"

"It was Jezza who set Mary up in the first place. Sold him out for fifty quid."

Del gave the money some side-eye. "And if I take the money and run?"

"We'll never do business again."

"Doing what?"

"I figure you've worked for more dealers than Yannis?"

He nodded.

"So you know the layout at some of these places? How many heavies are working the doors? Mebbe you know where they hide their stashes? Shit like that, right?"

An expression of understanding registered on Del's face, his eyes widened, and he grinned. "That's what you were doing at Yan's place."

"You catch on quick."

Del snatched the money out of my hand and added it to the rest of his stash. Then I handed him the heroin fentanyl mixture, which he hid with bird-quick precision.

"What the fuck you dickheads doing on our turf?"

The two Hilda's Boys from earlier had returned with a couple of identikit six foot bruisers with close-cropped hair and gym-honed arms adorned with ink. Now that he had a couple of big guys behind him, the ring leader grinned and came forward bravely.

"Yo, is your hearing fucked, bruv?"

"Sorry, gadge, moron isn't my first language — could you repeat the question in English?"

Del leaned into me.

"What the fuck're you doing?"

"Distracting them."

The ringleader, who looked like he'd just stumbled, punch-drunk, out of a Linkin Park concert in the nineties and decided that this was how he would dress for the rest of his life, took a step back, like he'd been slapped, and clicked his fingers at the skinhead closest to him. "Fuck this pussyhole up, Chuck."

The big guy stepped around the ring leader and came towards us. Despite me hissing at him to stand his ground, Del backed away in fear.

My brother emerged from one of the gardens about thirty feet behind the group with a nail encrusted baseball bat in his hands and stepped lightly in their direction. The men didn't notice, they were too busy watching the distraction.

Chuck removed a handle from his jeans pocket and unfurled a blade. He flashed a smile that was so full of hate it could have passed for a snarl.

"I'm gonna fuck you up."

I removed the pistol from my jacket and pointed it at him. "No mate, you've got that shit back-to-front."

He stopped smiling.

He started screaming when I put one in his left kneecap. His leg buckled, bent awkwardly, and cracked beneath him, making him shriek even louder.

His associates turned to run. The other bruiser ran straight into the baseball bat as my brother swung it into his shin. His leg snapped and he dropped with a cry of pain and started crawling along the tarmac.

The two remaining men chose different directions. Linkin' Park ran in our direction, then cut right towards the derelict houses. I put one in his left leg just as he reached one of the garden gates. He hit the deck with an agonised squeal

The other man tried to beat my brother for speed and attempted to rush past him. Derek slammed the bat into his right knee and tore it up. The man hopped on his good foot for a few seconds until my brother swung out again and destroyed that leg too.

Del looked around with jerky movements like he was expecting more of these pricks to emerge from the woodwork. When he realised that we were alone, he gave me a look of open-mouthed shock and tried to speak. I cut him off.

"I figured I'd kill two birds with one stone."

Raffles wanted revenge on Jezza, but he forgot about the pricks who put Mary on the slide in the first place: Hilda's Boys. If it wasn't for these idiots, Mary would still be Shawn Wilcox, would probably still be married, and would most likely have all his limbs. More importantly, he'd be alive.

I figured Raffles would appreciate what we were about to do. It was the kind of revenge he'd enjoy.

Del shook his head in disbelief at the carnage: four former tough guys screaming and weeping on bloody tarmac. "What a mess."

"It's about to get messier."

"I don't want nowt to do with this."

"Then you might wanna get the fuck outta here. Coz we're about to do some x-rated shit with these pricks. Besides, haven't you got summat you need to deliver?"

Del gave me a nod, then moved towards East Street without glancing back.

I pointed the gun at Linkin' Park, who cringed and whimpered. "Hope you boys are feeling brave, coz this shit's about to get scary."

"Fuck you, pussy," he replied. "You know who you're fuckin' with?"

"Yeah, some tit who's about to be hospitalised for a very long time."

That shut him up.

We dragged the pricks into one of the high-walled back gardens, closed the gate, and had some fun. We beat them with bricks until their faces looked like hamburger meat with eyes. Then we stripped them of their clothes and cash and left them to be collected by paramedics.

We didn't pull in a massive sum of money from our victims, but we earned more in that afternoon than we would have made from a month of retrieving debts for Piper.

That same evening, my brother took some unpaid leave, booked a flight to Ibiza for the following morning, and fought and fucked his way around the island for a month.

I waited around for a week.

I got the text on the Friday: "Package delivered."

I booked a flight to Amsterdam the very next day. I spent the week smoking weed and fucking European tourists. Piper warned me that if I stayed away for more than a week I wouldn't be welcomed back, so I got the train to Rotterdam and did another week of smoking and fucking. By the time I got home I could barely remember my name, and my cock felt like it had been through a meat grinder. It was probably the best fortnight of my life.

Piper welcomed me back with open arms and told me never to stay away so long again. He gave me cushy jobs delivering packages of cash to his many girlfriends and sent me to collect debts from the kinds of people who didn't put up much of a fight.

I forgot about Jezza.

My brother returned home from Ibiza with multiple bruises, numerous STIs, and a serious gambling habit. He quickly resettled into his old lifestyle and finally got his one-night stand with Janine Sterling.

Apparently, it was worth the wait.

A few weeks later I got a call from Del. It took me a few moments to remember who he was. "You been checking the papers recently?" he asked.

"No."

"Get your hands on last Friday's Gazette."

"Summat interesting in it?"

"Page three."

"Are there any tits on it?"

"After a fashion."

Then it dawned on me what he was talking about. I clutched the phone to my ear. "Is it done?"

"It took them two months to find him. Word has it that the Tango in his bloodstream killed the rats that tried to eat him. I know a gadgie in the police who said he looked like the Michelin Man's ugly brother."

"Nice image."

"Did you hear about Hilda's Boys?"

"No."

"After you packed off their compadres to the infirmary, the remaining Boys went scouring the area looking for someone to blame. They managed to force their way into Gary Feldman's place just as Bob Owden and Jimmy R were conducting some naughty business."

Bob Owden ran most of Teesside. If it was illegal and turned a profit, chances were good that most of that money would end up in Bob's pockets. Jimmy Raffin was his right-hand man, and dealt with most of his boss' problems via the old-fashioned methods of bloodshed and chaos.

"I bet that went well."

"If by well, you mean *really* fuckin' badly, then yeah, it was a complete success."

"Can't imagine Gaz was too happy that some silly fuckers tried storming his territory."

"It made what you did seem like a tickling from a feather duster. I heard they placed one of those silly bastards in the crusher while he was still alive. They told his friends to watch and learn."

That raised goosebumps. "Jesus."

"Yeah, I don't think He was around that day, and the upshot is that Bob's crew controls St Hilda's now."

"Okay."

"But there's a dealer on the outer edge of the area, who's not under Bob's protection. He runs a couple of junky squats. On a good day, he usually brings in about five to ten grand."

This news jacked my heart-rate. I'd been waiting for something more interesting to do than being Piper's delivery boy.

Maybe this was it.

"Do you know the layout?"

"Not yet, but I reckon I can find out."

"Ten percent."

"Twenty."

"Final offer of fifteen."

"You've got a deal."

I smiled. The Stanton brothers were back in business.

The Stanton brothers' stories arranged in chronological order from the earliest occurring tale in the timeline to latest:

A Man Called Mary (part of *Six Shooter*)
Fighting Talk
Bad Luck and Trouble
Best Laid Plans
The Beautiful Game (part of *Dirty Snow and other stories*)
The Greatest Show in Town (part of *Dirty Snow and other stories*)
The Green-eyed Monster
Bone Breakers
Dirty Snow (part of *Dirty Snow and other stories*)
Noughts and Double Crosses
One-Sixteenth (part of *Dirty Snow and other stories*)
The Fight (part of *Dirty Snow and other stories*)
The Hunters
The Glasgow Grin

MARTIN STANLEY

Printed in Great Britain
by Amazon

49239813R00106